HUGO

How Two Boys Learned of Life

From a Killer Shark

By Michael McEachern

To my wonderful wife, who has given me decades of love and forgiveness.

Table of Contents

A FUNERAL

The funeral of Russell Wainwright, though only a graveside service, included a military honor guard and a twenty-one-gun salute. After a homily by the minister of Beaufort's First Baptist Church, several friends spoke. The first was a retired Army lieutenant general for whom Russell had served as radioman in Viet Nam when the general was a lieutenant colonel. He was strong in his praise, listing Russell's many sterling qualities.

In conclusion, he said something memorable. He said he'd seen Russell nearly undone on more than one occasion over the loss of special friends, but he had never -- not once -- ever seen him afraid. "In fact, it was his willingness to put himself in harm's way to support his men that led me to choose him as my radioman. He saved many lives and more than a few precarious situations. I've served with many brave soldiers," he said in conclusion, "but only then-Sergeant Wainwright was -- at least it seemed to me -- entirely without fear."

Another speaker, Michael Mixon, told of the childhood he'd shared with Russell, and of one time when he and Russell had climbed onto the roof of a three-story house. Mixon said he was terrified, couldn't remember what had caused him to do such a thing. While he clung to a central chimney he kept trying to hide his fear by talking to his friend in what he hoped was a normal tone of voice. Receiving no answer, he summoned the courage to turn his face away from the reassuring masonry to locate his partner in foolishness. He said that he had nearly thrown up when he saw Wainwright standing on the very edge of the roof, then jumping across ten feet of empty space to grab onto the limb of a pecan tree. Mixon said he had to agree with the general: Wainwright had been a fearless fellow. In fact, he knew of a time when Russell's nerves had failed him, but a funeral was not the place for that story.

PART ONE

1. A GIANT SHARK

"**P**robably another hour," Russ said. "Why don't we walk down to Sires and get a candy bar. I could sure use a Zero."

"Does it seem like tide's slower than usual today? Mikey asked.

"Seems to me like it's stopped."

The boys left the river shore and walked the two short blocks to Sires Gulf Station at the corner of Port Republic and Carteret Streets. They charged a couple of candy bars and two RC Cola's to the account of Russ's dad. Back at the river the tide didn't look like it had moved even a foot closer to the boat.

"Damn," Mikey said, "this is ridiculous. Let's just get in the mud and push it out. We'll be here all day at this rate."

They doubled the bows of their sneakers and bogged out to the boat. The mud in this creek was the color of a wet cigar, firm enough to support hundreds of fiddler holes, but so soft the boys sank to their knees. Each step required tugging the rear foot out of its hole against the suction of the warm mud, and the breaking vacuum spoke bowel sounds. The boat was a beat up 14-foot plywood Halsey skiff with an 18-horse Johnson, also beat up. Mikey had carried the anchor and line from shore and he stowed it in the bow. It wasn't hard for them both to spin the boat so that the bow faced the incoming tide. They set the oars under the transom and used them as levers. In a few minutes the boat was in the shallows. They fetched their cooler of beer, Thermos of water and a bag of Vienna sausage, sardines and potato chips. The fishing gear was always left in the boat. They poled out of the creek to the river, then hung their feet over the side and washed the mud off, started the old Johnson and got underway.

Russ and Mikey had been friends since the first grade, eight years ago, and this summer they were spending a lot of time in the river. They'd built 45 crab pots and ran them every day except Sunday. Every day but Sunday, Blue Channel Company -- the outfit that bought all the local crabs -- sent two boats out from their plant in Port Royal to buy the crabbers' catch. The *Miss Mary* bought Russ and Mikey's crabs. She ran north, from Port Royal to Edisto Island and back. The other boat went south. Russ and Mikey had an old sixteen-foot bateau with a twenty-five-horse Johnson they used to run the pots. They'd stay in the river every morning waiting for the *Miss Mary*. As soon as she came into sight, they'd ease into her path and Captain Charlie would throttle back to an idle. They'd pull alongside and Russ would fix the bow line to a cleat, then hand bushel baskets of crabs up to Captain Charlie, a huge black man with a single gold tooth in the very front of his otherwise perfect teeth, an ornament he always displayed as part of his broad and irrepressible smile.

Occasionally, if the weather was bad or *Miss Mary* needed Captain Charlie's tending, a young black helper would collect the baskets. Then both crab magnates would climb aboard to transact business. Charlie would weigh the crabs on a rusty Fairbanks platform scale. He'd ask how much bait the boys needed, then deduct the bait charge from the crab pay. A receipt was written and payment was made in cash money on the spot. In those days crabs were bringing five-and-a-half cents a pound; bait was three cents for menhaden, two-and-a-half for croaker. The plant only sent croaker if they ran out of menhaden. Croaker didn't catch near as well as menhaden, so nobody liked it. *Miss Mary* also carried a store of salted bull nose for the few fellows who still ran trotlines. The bait fish and the bull nose gave *Miss Mary* the strong organic smell of flesh and guts, acrid, but not unpleasant.

Running pots and selling crabs was done usually by 9:30 or 10:00, so the rest of the day was theirs to do whatever. Mikey would have to cut the grass every other week and clean and wax the wood floors of his house once a month. Russ would occasionally have to work at his family's dry cleaners. But mostly the boys did what they wanted. They went down the river two or three times a week. They'd usually go on Saturdays because with no crabbing to do Sundays they could stay overnight. Their parents were always agreeable. If the weather turned bad or if mechanical problems developed and the boys had to stay an extra night, the parents didn't worry. More than one extra night would cause some alarm, but so far that had never happened.

Together with several friends they had built a rough camp on a deepwater creek about five minutes from the ocean, a 16' x 24' shed with a propane cookstove, a sink and some shelving for cooking supplies. The cooking area was walled off from the bunkroom, which was just screened in. In the winter they'd let down blinds of heavy duck nailed along the top edges to the upper framework of the walls and to a 2x2 along the bottom edges. These would be rolled up to facilitate stowing the canvas in warm weather or when light was wanted more than heat. On winter nights this arrangement did a pretty fair job of keeping a little warmth in.

The first time they ever saw the giant they later named Hugo the boys were anchored maybe 100 yards outside the breakers of Bay Point Island's south end, fishing for shark. Bay Point is the first barrier island north of Hilton Head, and just south of Capers Island. They'd caught their bait -- a small mess of medium shrimp and a half-dozen finger mullet -- throwing the cast net in Morse Island Creek just before yesterday's low tide. Russ was laid across the forward seat, his head resting on a floatation cushion that looked custom-made for the boat, faded dull gray-green, torn in places, one strap connected on one end and the other missing entirely. He was smoking a cigarette. Mikey was similarly composed on the aft, or driver's seat, but without the cigarette. His cushion looked to be of a slightly more recent vintage, with straps fastened at both ends. The rigs were tending themselves, the rod tips protruding outboard of the gunnels about a foot, the heels of the rods resting on the boat's bottom where it joined the sides. A Carling Black Label rested on the floor in each boy's half-opened hand. Mikey raised his beer a couple of inches and concluded it was too empty to have any chill left in it. He tossed it over his head into the water and sat up to get another.

"Jesus! Wainwright, sit up!"

Russ came alive quickly, sat up and followed Mikey's pointing finger. "God-damn," he barely spoke, to himself mainly.

Off toward the beach, not more than twenty-five yards, and cruising lazily on a direct course to the stern of the boat was the largest shark the boys had ever seen, probably the largest they would ever see. Russ reached under the bow and grabbed the boat's shark dispatcher, a sawed-off 12-gauge single shot, fairly rusted from end to end by the salt air, but always loaded with either 00 buckshot or slugs. He broke it open to check the load, then handed it to Mikey. The gun was highly effective at point blank range, with the shark gaffed and pulled alongside the boat, its head barely covered with water, or not at all, but here, even if the beast swam within three feet of the boat, half a dorsal fin's depth might be protection enough. Plus, this creature's skin would make an alligator's hide seem like a baby's bottom. Mikey took his eyes away from the casually approaching monster long enough to appraise the rusty 12-guage, aware suddenly of how small it was.

Whether it was the sound of the commotion in the boat or some interesting sight or scent requiring investigation, the shark turned ninety degrees to starboard and eased off toward Hilton Head, nearly paralleling the Bay Point beach and leaving the boat behind. Still in no hurry. Russ had been retrieving his line as quickly as he could, hoping to cast ahead of the fish if it passed out of range of the 12-gauge and maybe get it to strike the finger mullet. He'd kept his eyes glued to the shark, though, and now he felt the extra weight of his rig clearing the water. As he set his rod in the boat, he noticed nothing had touched his bait. A minute passed in silence, as both boys stared at the gradually vanishing apparition. Finally Mikey turned his eyes away, opened the cooler and took out two beers. He had to press the can against Russ's arm to get his attention. Tied to a small rusty screw eye, a church key hung from a short length of cotton twine forward of each seat. Both boys sat and opened their beers in silence.

Russ spoke. "Mikey, I believe I've swum my last swim."

2. UPGRADING THE RIGS

B ack in town Mikey dropped Russ at the anchoring site they'd left that morning, then headed to the landing where the crab boat was moored. Russ brought his car, a rusty but reliable old '50 model Chevy, around. They'd tied up to the bateau, so there'd be no lost time next day. The bateau was kept tethered to a mooring buoy, with an anchor line running to high ground. They normally didn't keep their fishing skiff there because it was a lot farther from where they fished. But tomorrow, as soon as they'd finished crabbing, they'd jump right in the Halsey and head out. The tide would be nearly an hour later coming up tomorrow than it had been today and they didn't want to twiddle their thumbs.

With the boat secure, they carried empty gas cans to the car and headed to town. Besides the gas, the boys wanted to upgrade their shark rigs. They talked about going all out and buying one of the chain-leader shark hooks sold at Fordham's Hardware store. These were mammoth 19-ought hooks with three-foot link chain leaders. The hook was well over a foot long and had a 6-inch gap between the barb and the ½" diameter shaft. They went to Fordham's to ogle the rig. The store owner came to ask if he could help.

Mikey spoke up, "Mr. Fordham, what do you think you would bait this thing with, a ham?"

"A nice size bass or sheepshead would be enough. Thing is, if you hooked something big enough to take the bait, what then?"

"We'd get him in somehow," said Russ. "What do people who buy them do?"

"Truth is, Russell, I've never sold a one of these rigs. Notice I've only got the one. I keep it because it's a curiosity; people come in just to see it. I expect if I ever sell one it'll be to decorate some retired fisherman's wall somewhere.

The boys left the rig on the wall. They knew it wasn't too big, but maybe they didn't need anything that size. Besides, it was a lot of money. If they lost it they'd feel pretty low for a while, they reckoned. Plus, the hooks they'd been using would probably stand more pulling than they could. But they didn't want to go the next day without some upgrade. Finally, they decided to get larger hooks, 12-ought Mustads, 6" long with about 2" separating the barb from the ¼" shaft. They were affordable. Mikey had the idea they should use a piece of porch swing chain he had laying about as a leader, so they cut the near-eight-foot piece in half and tied the four-foot leaders to each of the new hooks using a heavy stainless fishing leader and galvanized swivels between the hook and the chain. Now, for not too much money, they had much heavier rigs than what they'd had before.

While they assembled the new tackle, they talked about the shark.

"How long do you think he was, really? I mean he looked like twenty feet to me, but do sharks really get that big?" Mikey asked Russ.

"He was at <u>least</u> twenty feet. He was way longer than the Halsey."

"Maybe he's a whale shark. I think I've heard of something called a whale shark. Big as he is, it seems like maybe he's one."

Well, I never heard of a whale shark, but if there's such a thing this might be one," Russ allowed. "You ought to check the encyclopedia."

"Yeah, good idea. I wonder how much he weighs? And if we hook him, then what? I'm not so sure we can land such a fish."

"Well, first things first. We've got to find him again before we can hook him."

"Do you think it's likely to be there again tomorrow?" asked Mikey.

Russ wasn't optimistic. "We've never seen him before. I wouldn't be surprised if we never see him again. Still, we gotta try. Man, what a trophy he'd make! People won't believe it."

"I wonder if Mr. Fischer would buy him. Maybe he's too big. Probably be like chewing leather."

"We need to name him. We can't have such a monster swimming around without a name."

Eventually Russ hit on Hugo and Mikey liked it. It seemed to possess an unknown-but-scary quality.

3. CAPTAIN CHARLIE

The next morning the boys were done running pots before nine o'clock. They were too anxious to wait around for the *Miss Mary*, so they loaded the crabs into the Halsey and set out south. They saw Captain Charlie just before *Miss Mary* reached the Lady's Island Bridge, but waited for him to pass under the draw before going alongside. The incoming tide could complicate things if *Miss Mary* was stern to it when the two boats passed under the draw. This way there was plenty of room. Charlie hailed them as Russ threw him the bow line. He was beaming, as usual. "You boys using the offshore racer for crabbin' this morning?"

Russ started handing up the baskets of crabs. "Yeah, she's an offshore racer alright. The bottom flexes like a cotton sheet in a stiff breeze if we hit the wake of a rowboat. One rib's split and we got a half dozen leaks. If we had good sense, we'd keep it on the trailer, not use it to chase down monster sharks."

"Oh, so that's what the boat rods and heavy tackle is for. And chain leader! You must be expecting a monster sure enough."

When all the crabs were loaded Russ jumped aboard *Miss Mary*, Mikey right behind him. "Charlie," Mikey said, "we saw a shark off Bay Point yesterday that HAD to be twenty feet long.

"Maybe TWENTY-FIVE!" said Russell.

"That's no joke! What do you think? You think we'd had too much Black Label?"

Charlie laughed. "Y'all ain't drank all that stuff up yet?"

Russ answered, "I almost wish we had. We still got maybe sixty cases to go. Want some?"

"Well thank you, but no, I'm partial to gin myself." Charlie finished weighing the crabs. "How much bait?"

Mikey spoke up, "Give us a whole box. We'll use some for chum, maybe bait our hooks with it, too, if it don't look too bad."

"No, it looks real good this morning. We musta got some fresh in last night." Charlie called his helper in the wheelhouse and the boy tied the wheel and went aft for the menhaden. The bait came in 50-pound wooden boxes, but for some reason "a box" was 100 pounds. Mikey climbed back down into the Halsey. The boy handed down one box, then went for the second one. By the time Mikey had the first box stowed, the boy was back with the second. Mikey stowed it atop the first, then climbed back aboard *Miss Mary*.

Mikey asked Charlie again, "So do you think that shark was just our imagination, or what?"

Charlie had finished writing the receipt and now he counted the cash into Mikey's hand from a well-worn zippered bank bag. "No, I wouldn't say that. Truth is, you just don't never know what's down there. Y'all ever know Itch Robinson? No? Well, he used to trotline not too far from where your pots are now. This was maybe ten years ago. His first summer crabbin' Itch keeps seeing these great big shadows pass under his boat when he's crossin' deep water to get to the shore where he likes to set his line. Devilfish, you know. We've all seen them at times, usually in bigger water, though. St. Helena's good for 'em. Port Royal, too, but not so much as St. Helena. But Itch never had. Swore to me he'd never even heard of 'em. So he decides he's going to catch one. He rigs up a harpoon with about 100' of the cheapest rope he can find. I never saw the rig myself; I was running the south route back then. Shaft was just an ole giggin' handle. Had a friend make the head from an old anchor. People say it looked pretty good.

"Anyway, Itch takes this harpoon with him every day when he goes to crab. And don't you know one day a great big devilfish passes right under his boat. And Itch is quick enough to stick it with his harpoon. Well, now the fun begins... Itch manages not to get himself tangled up in the disappearing line, manages to hang on until his boat is up to devilfish cruising speed, which lucky for Itch ain't fast. The fish apparently has in mind visiting St. Helena, so Itch just has to hang on. He knows his hands won't stand much of this duty, so he takes a couple of wraps around his bow cleat and just sets back. Dreamin' of glory, no doubt. Well, he stuck his fish just south of Pigeon Point early in the morning. Tide is going out, so when the fish heads toward St. Helena Itch figures this'll be short work, bucking the current and all. In a mile or so he passes Pleasant Point, another mile and he's at the air base fuel dock. When he passes Brickyard Point boat landing he realized he's passed the tide divide and he's now moving right along, the fish with the tide at his back. No sign his pull is slacknin'.

"Itch rides that fish all morning and into the afternoon: way out St. Helena Sound, some miles out. Then the fish turns south, heads for Savannah, or Miami, who knows. Not Itch, that's for sure. He finally figures that if he cuts loose right then he can make it back to someplace before dark. 'Course Itch ain't got no motor. But the weather cooperated and tide changed in time for him to make it back to Port Royal Sound and back to Beaufort. It was dark long before he got home. He didn't run his line the next day.

So no, I got no problem believin' you saw such a fish. But just remember Itch before you go castin' out in front of it."

4. A LARGE SHARK, BUT NOT HUGO

The boys went back to where they were the day before, but a little closer to the shore. The ocean was calm and the sky was clear. Dozens of seabirds walked the beach near the boat, too far away to see in detail, but clearly the same little ones seen on every beach, speed walking from morsel to morsel, tiny stiff-legged robots. Peck the water's edge, run four, five or ten feet, legs, even when observed close-up, just a blur. Peck again. 6-volt birds running on 12-volt batteries.

They set out their lines and chummed the water with the menhaden. They drank beer and Russ smoked. In the air an occasional small formation of pelicans passed, sometimes near; otherwise nothing but seagulls, coming in for the chum. Soon the boys cut back on the chumming, not wanting to waste expensive bait on flying rats. Gradually the beer and sun took the edge off their vigilance and both boys reclined on their seats just like the day before, beers at hand. Occasionally Mikey stirred himself to get more beers, then he'd check the water in the bilge and if it was more than an inch deep he'd bail it out with an old Spam can. There was a big coffee can, too, to bail rainwater.

By noon the tide had risen to nearly full and a gentle easterly breeze picked up. Small waves were breaking on the shore, hardly visible from the boat except for the narrow foam bands they formed, lazing a few yards up the shallow beach.

Russ had just checked and re-baited his line with a fresh menhaden -- the previous one was half eaten, probably by crabs -- when he noticed a disturbance in the water a short distance to the seaward side of the boat. His cast fell just a few feet wide, but before he'd even set the clicker on his reel, the line started paying out. Engaging the clicker gave sound to the run and the sound was a scream. The line was peeling off the spool at a rate that would use all 300 yards of the 50-pound test long before the fish tired. Russ began tightening the star drag while Mikey hoisted the anchor and retrieved his own rig. With the drag almost to max the boat began to come around to the pull of the fish. Mikey started the engine and followed the fish slowly, just fast enough to slow the clicker to an almost countable ticking. The fish headed directly out, away from the beach. After a few minutes Russ turned the star drag until it stopped; that was all the resistance the reel could provide, and it was enough to silence the clicker. After another couple of minutes Mikey knocked the 18-horse into neutral, increasing the load on the fish and causing the line to pay out slowly, the ticking once again nearly countable. After another few minutes the clicking stopped; the fish was tiring.

The boys had never hooked a fish that pulled like this and they were sure they'd hooked into Hugo on their first time hunting him. The fish had begun to zig and zag, his course no longer directly offshore, but still generally so. Mikey bumped the engine into reverse, and the ticking started again, the line paying out slowly, but too fast for the clicks to be counted. Within a minute, though, the clicks had stopped again. Mikey shut the motor down; now it was time for Russ to begin working the fish in, a turn or three of the reel handle at a time. Standing before the front seat, thighs hard against the frame of the bow's cover, Russ would pull back on the boat rod until it was vertical, then quickly reel in as much as he could while letting the rod fall to horizontal.

Close along South Carolina's coast mud suspended in the tidal outflows from the rivers, sounds and innumerable small inlets makes the ocean murky. It took nearly two hours to get the fish close enough to see him, at first just a shadow well beneath the surface. They'd been pulled far enough out from shore that the water was pretty clear. Mikey said, "How'd you like to be swimming along, bi-valve happy, and look down and catch a glimpse of that."

Russ took up the thought, "...then see it turn to the surface and rocket right at you, not just a scary shape anymore, now you know exactly what it is." He finished his sketch with a short bugling of the first three bars of Taps.

Mikey said, "Yeah, I'm done with swimming too."

After a couple more minutes the fish could be seen, not clearly yet, but clearly enough. Russ said, "Well, if we get it in the boat it'll be the biggest we ever caught, but it sure ain't old Hugo."

Mikey agreed, "But it might go ten or twelve feet."

When brought close enough to allow Mikey to get a gaff in, the fish had sufficient strength left to snatch the gaff away and nearly pull the gaffer after it. It spit the gaff right away but Mikey was able to retrieve it using one of the oars. Russ brought the struggling fish around again and this time Mikey managed to gaff it and hang on. The 12-gauge had been brought out early and set on the front seat. Russ was able to grab the gun with his right hand while holding his rod with his left. The shark was ideally positioned for a point-blank shot through the top of the head and Russ didn't hesitate. In an instant the creature was inert.

After wrestling with the fish for fifteen minutes and nearly being swamped by the low swells a half-dozen times, the boys concluded that to get the beast into the boat they would have to go to the shore where they could get some real purchase and not risk capsizing their leaky craft. They secured the fish as best they could to the side of the boat and made the slow trip toward the south end of the island where a small cut fills from half-flood up, forming a quarter-moon of several hundred yards extent, sand on the beach side, tall green marshgrass and mud on the inland side.

After finding a site of suitable firmness and flatness on the sand side, the boys jumped into the shallow water and managed, using the oars as levers, to pry, hoist and tug, push and pull, and otherwise plain worry to get the shark aboard. The boat was obviously now overloaded, so the boys took some pains to distribute the weight in a way calculated to minimize the chance the craft would swamp. The head rested on the back seat opposite Mikey with the body filling the boat more or less diagonally, the tail protruding above the bow and tied off as close to centerline as possible with a length of rope secured to the bow cleat. The overall length was something over twelve feet, far and away the boys' lifetime biggest.

Russ joked, "I'm glad you got the business end of this beast. If he wakes up it'll be your leg not mine."

"Thanks for the concern, partner. If he wakes up, though, we'll both be swimming with him. He'd break this boat to pieces getting free of the ropes. But he's dead as a hammer."

"Yeah, that's what Sam Keyserling thought about that alligator he killed on the road back from Charleston, remember?"

"Damn, I wish you hadn't reminded me of that."

A friend of Russ's older brother Bobby, Sam Keyserling, had been on his way back to Beaufort from Charleston early one night when a small alligator appeared in his headlights. The gator was less than five feet long and appeared to have been run over. Sam figured he could skin it and make something from the hide. He'd never done such a thing, but figured he could learn. So he stopped in the highway, backed up to put the animal in the full brightness of his lights, and got out. There were no wounds apparent; the skin would be perfect. His trunk was stuffed with stereo equipment, so he'd have to put the critter in the back seat. Fearing the gator might only be stunned and might possibly awaken, Sam pulled a 22 caliber Ruger Bearcat revolver from his glove box and put a long rifle hollow point into the gator's head, point-blank. That little hole he figured he could repair. He then covered the back seat with a beach towel and some dirty clothes to protect the upholstery, just in case the animal bled. These precautions taken, he threw the alligator in the back seat and continued on his way home.

He made it past Lobeco and almost to the Whale Branch bridge before the reptile awoke, in a bad mood. The first Sam knew of his predicament, the gator's tail slammed into the back of his seat throwing him against the steering wheel and nearly causing him to have a heart attack. Terrified, he jammed his brakes and whipped the car off the pavement and onto the causeway shoulder. The deceleration threw the alligator off the seat and onto the floor. Sam could hear the reptile hissing and could feel his flailing tail working under the front seat. He opened his door and leapt from the car before it had come to a full stop. The car continued to roll, picking up a little speed as it followed the falling slope of the shoulder leading to the mud, marshgrass and water of the north shore of Whale Branch. Tide was full high. By the time the car hit the water it was moving fast enough to leave the hard sand completely and drift a few feet from the causeway's edge before the open door caused it to settle quickly to the mud, leaving only the roof and windows above the water.

Russ said, "You guess how much this critter weighs, I'll do the same? Closest wins five dollars."

"I'm not about to bet five dollars, but I'll go a six pack of Pabst, if you drive the boat back."

"Deal."

The idea of a non-Black Label six-pack was pretty enticing. The boys had been drinking Carling for months now, ever since the beer warehouse at the end of Depot Road had caught fire and burned nearly down. Thousands of cans had exploded. Most everything else was damaged beyond saving or at least beyond selling. Some cans were scorched so badly you couldn't tell what the contents might be. Others showed no sign of the fire. The fire had happened at night and word had come to Russ immediately via his mother whose best friend worked as a telephone operator. On hearing the sirens, Mrs. Wainwright picked up the phone and got the news. Within twenty minutes Russ and Mikey were on site with the old Chevy gathering loot.   They worked hours and relayed loads to Mikey's garage, a dilapidated clapboard structure with a dirt floor. It had never been used in the years since Mikey's folks had bought the property. They ended with something over 1,800 cans of beer. Some of it was okay, but most of it smelled bad. It all worked, though.

Russ said, "Okay, pick a number."

"375 pounds."

Russ didn't hesitate a second. "I'll say 376."

Russ would always do an over/under on a bet if he could. Mikey didn't mind; he gave his best guess, so he'd be as likely to bet a pound more as a pound less if he had to choose another number. But he never let Russ choose the amount at risk; he knew better than that.

The trip back was a little dicey, despite good weather. The boat wallowed under the extra weight and it began to leak faster than usual, the boys figured from the strain the weight put on the seams as the little boat, following the seas, crossed the swells at any attitude but dead-on. Russ gradually worked his way out into the sound far enough to allow him to keep the skiff at ninety degrees to the waves. He would position the boat on the back of a swell and vary the engine's power to stay there. That way the strain was minimized and the leaking slowed.

5. THE CRAB FACTORY

The boys took their catch to the crab factory. There it could be unloaded by hydraulic winch winding wire rope through the sheaves of a davit. When they pulled up to the dock, Blue Channel's dock-and-steamer manager, a black man about seven feet tall named David Simmons, better known as Captain Dave, came to the end to help unload. Strangely, if he were by himself David Simmons looked like an ordinary man from a distance, so well-proportioned was his overlarge frame. It was only when a person approached him that his size dawned. When Captain Dave looked over the edge and saw the cargo, he whistled. "You boys ain't got a single lick of sense, not one brain into your entire head, neither one of you. That fish bigger'n your boat. S'pose he'd figured that out? Then what?"

Mikey answered, "That wouldn't have been good, Cap'm Dave, but I guess we were counting on fish not figurin'."

"Well, you youngstas keep countin' like that an' it's gonna get you some short change one day. You want me to hoist 'm up?"

Captain Dave sent down the cable with a pair of hooks attached to short chains at the end. Normally this rig was used to lift 55-gallon drums of crabs onto the dock. Lots of crabbers -- most, really -- used 55-gallon drums, not baskets, to take the crabs to market. All the crab drums had their empty weight written in crude white spray paint and all had a hole burned into either side, just below the drum's lip, for the hooks. Because the davit had been designed and built to lift these drums, its height was just adequate for that task. In order that the shark clear the edge of the dock, Russ fashioned a sling from one of the skiff's docklines forming an eye in the middle by tying a bowline on the bight formed by doubling enough of the line for that purpose, then secured one leg of the sling around the tail end and the other around the torso where the head's set on the seat allowed easy access, using timber hitches in both cases. When he gave the go-ahead, Captain Dave brought the fish on up to the dock. Tied head and tail, the shark cleared the dock, but it still nearly dragged, so it couldn't be set on a pair of platform rollers like were used to move the crab barrels from the head of the dock to the steaming shed. That had been Russ's plan when he tied the sling. Instead, they had to untie and re-tie the shark and drag it down the dock. Russ and Mikey dragged it over halfway unassisted, then Captain Dave took mercy on the boys and gave a hand. He could have done the job without help.

Once the fish was in the shade of the steamer shed, Russ borrowed the phone and called the fish market that was located just about a half-mile farther up the same creek as Blue Channel. He told Mr. Fischer, the owner, what they had and struck a deal for $25. It was less than the boys had hoped, but it was something. They'd been afraid the market might not buy it at all because of its size. The boys waited for the fish market pickup to arrive with their money. It was there in five minutes, Mr. Fischer and a strong young helper. The helper went right to work with a razor-sharp gutting knife and a machete. Slitting the belly and removing the guts went quickly, but when the young man tried to reduce the carcass to manageable portions with the machete he found tough going. The first swing, just behind the head, didn't even cut through the skin, the second barely did. He set the machete on the truck's tailgate and went to the cab. In a second he was back with a largish bastard file and began working the edge of the machete. After a minute or so, he felt the keenness with his thumb, put the file away and went back to work, this time with more success.

"We got a little bet going, Mr. Fischer," Russ told the shop owner. "Weight. We need to have the total weight."

Fischer was okay with that request. "It's got to be cut up anyway."

Russ thought he might get more action. "For five dollars, what do you think he weighs, Mr. Fischer?"

"I don't bet, Russ, but I'd say 500 pounds. That's not a bet now."

Russ nodded. "I'd say 499, but I know you're not betting."

The guts were loaded into a #3 washtub, weighed on Captain Dave's platform scale, the same model as on the *Miss Mary*, and thrown into the back of the pickup. The meat portions, as they were cut, were likewise weighed. The shark weighed out at 470 pounds. Russ looked to Mikey for an acknowledgment of the weight and Mikey nodded okay. Mr. Fischer gave Russ five five-dollar bills, asked if they would hose off the mess to Captain Dave's satisfaction, thanked the boys for the business and left. He hadn't been there fifteen minutes. Captain Dave fetched a stiff-bristle broom for Mikey and while Russ hosed the bloody concrete Mikey scrubbed off the congealed traces that had outlined the pools of blood. In a very little while Captain Dave pronounced the job well done.

The boys just idled on the trip back to town. That way talk was easier. Mikey stated the obvious. "That shark was about all we can handle, rigged like we are. And it's nothing compared to Hugo. I think we need to invest in a couple of floating sets using the big rigs Fordham's has."

"Yeah, I think you're right, but even if the floating rigs do all the work, even if the shark is drowned when we get there, if it's Hugo we've got to come up with another way to get him home."

6. SHARK FLOTATION

The solution to the shark transportation problem, thought out on the trip back, involved two inner tubes and a fire extinguisher.   They planned to get Mr. Fordham to order a second rig just like the one on the wall. They could pay for both with the shark money and have a little left. They could get the inner tubes from old man Griffin's filling station for free because they didn't have to be good; they both knew how to patch inner tubes.   The other expense would be the fire extinguisher, rather two fire extinguishers if they could afford them.

The next morning when they met *Miss Mary* they found their shark catch was on the grapevine, at least the Blue Channel grapevine. Captain Charlie greeted them by doffing his captain's cap and hailing them "Good morning anglers.   Where is the offshore racer today? I hope this means I can tell Captain Dave you're giving up on the leviathan. He's worried we're about to lose our highliners. The Company needs you boys."

Russ was handing up the baskets. "We got to make a few changes is all. We'll be back to business tomorrow."

7. MR. ZOO

When they got back to the hill they set out first for Fordham's. They bought the rig off the wall and asked Mr. Fordham to order a second, identical one. Mr. Fordham said he'd order two more, not wanting to lose one of the attractions of his store's fishing section. They checked out fire extinguishers while there, but the only CO_2 models were way too large. The idea of the shark transport rig was to have it available without taking up a lot of space. Next, they went to Griffin's and found two nearly perfect tubes from 20-inch truck tires. They then went to NAPA and bought a goodly quantity of tire patch material and glue. So outfitted, they took themselves and their materials to Mr. Zoo's shop off Carteret Street.

Mr. Zoo was a machinist mainly, but he could do pretty nearly anything of a practical nature. He let the boys use his workbench when he wasn't busy on it, and gave them pointers on their work. When he heard the boys' shark fishing plan, he was interested. Russ went out to the Chevy and retrieved the newly purchased hook and chain. He handed it over to Mr. Zoo for his appraisal. "This must be some big fish. How do you plan to land him?"

Mikey said, "We hope he'll wear himself out, maybe drown, fighting a five-gallon float."

Mr. Zoo thought a second. "You two should go see Everett Paul. You might not know him -- he's old now -- but he lives just down from you, Michael, that three-story place just across Federal Street from the Castle. On the little lake. He lives on the ground floor. Years back he did some serious big-fish fishing. Maybe sharks, too, I don't know. Offshore. He might have some good ideas for you. I know he'd like to be asked. Go see him. He drives a green GMC pickup with a pipe rack. If the truck's there, he's home."

The boys told Mr. Zoo they would, then described to him the shark portage rig they'd dreamt up. They planned to cut each of their inner tubes clean across, fairly near the valve stem, making each tube into a "U", then glue the cuts closed, so the U would hold air. They would remove the valves from the stems so they could be filled quickly using a CO_2 fire extinguisher. They'd modify the fire extinguisher by removing the discharge horn, leaving only a rigid pipe which could be pressed over the mouth of the tube's valve stem. They would rely on the valve stem screw-on caps to keep the tubes from leaking air.

Mr. Zoo was skeptical. "How you going to make sure the fish doesn't come out of the U?"

Russ said he could tie him in somehow. "We'll rig something."

Zoo was unimpressed with the plan. "Look boys, jury-rigs are fine if they're needed because something unexpected comes up. But not now when there's plenty of time to figure it out. Let me suggest a minor modification of the tube U's. We make up a pair of wooden clamps to squeeze the glued ends closed. Put five through-bolts through each pair, and on bolt number three -- the center one -- we set a threaded eye. Now, we can be more confident the air pressure won't tear your glued seams open and you've got a convenient and secure way to lash your tubes tight around the fish, and also to tow him in, just in case your hook works loose. By the way, even using the clamps, I'd caution you to use as little air as will float your catch. You also might take two spare tubes. 'Most anything you catch will fit through a 20" tube, and you can tie those easily without extra hardware."

Russ and Mikey were impressed. Russ said, "I got to admit, that's a WAY lot better than what I didn't have in mind."

They went right to work on the project. It took most of two hours to create, even with Mr. Zoo's help, but it looked great when they finished. Mr. Zoo had all the stuff they needed, even some scraps of lumber for the clamps. Mikey asked what they owed him, but he waved them off. Russ said, "We gotta at least pay you for the nuts and bolts."

Mr. Zoo took his pencil from behind his ear and did a quick calculation on a remnant of the wood they'd used. "Okay," he said, "eighty-five cents."

Russ paid and the boys gathered up their new gear, thanked Mr. Zoo, and headed over to see Everett Paul. The GMC was not at the house, so they went on in search of a small CO_2 extinguisher. There was a second hardware store in town, but it had no CO_2 extinguishers at all. Moore's Welding had a couple of CO_2 extinguishers, but they were bigger even than the model Fordham's had. Mikey asked Mr. Moore where he bought his extinguishers and the old man took the time to get the name of the business and the telephone number. It was in Savannah, though. Long distance. Still, there was little choice.

Since all the parents had a very negative reaction to long distance calling, they got change for three dollars and went to a pay phone. When Mikey asked the clerk at the fire extinguisher store whether they had a small CO_2 extinguisher, something that would only be maybe fifteen inches tall and say three to six inches in diameter, he was pleased to hear that such an extinguisher was in stock. They would hold it if the boys planned to drive over; otherwise they delivered to Beaufort twice a month and the next scheduled delivery was the coming Friday. They could drop it at Moore's Welding if the boys would leave the money there or if Mr. Moore was willing to put it on his account. The price was $12.95, plus 3% tax. Mikey thanked the lady and said they'd call back.

"Damn," Mikey said when he'd hung up, "they cost over thirteen dollars. That's more than the hook rig. We need to think."

8. MR. PAUL

They rode by Everett Paul's house again and this time the GMC was in the yard. When they went to knock on the door they found it open and could see through the screen an old man standing at the kitchen sink. "Mr. Paul?" Mikey called.

The old man turned around to face the door. "You got him."

Mikey introduced himself and Russ. "Mr. Zoo told us you might be able to give us some help, or some ideas anyway. We're trying to catch a huge shark. Mr. Zoo said you'd done a lot of fishing for big fish."

"Many years ago. Zoo doing okay? I haven't seen him in probably three months."

"Yes, sir," Mikey answered. "He's doing fine. So what kind of fishing did you do?"

"Mostly billfish and Tuna, but I landed some fairly large shark. Come on back to the living room. Want a glass of iced tea, water?"

"Tea would be great, if it's no trouble," said Russ. Mikey seconded the tea request. Mr. Paul opened a cupboard beside the sink and pulled out two jelly glasses, then went to the refrigerator, got an ice tray from the frozen section and cracked the ice with a wooden pestle. He put ice in both glasses and filled them with tea.

He talked as he poured. "The biggest was a hammerhead over sixteen feet long.

Fishing out of Miami near the Gulf Stream. Seen bigger ones, but that's the biggest one I caught. You ever seen a shark that size?"

"Mr. Paul, we're pretty sure we saw one much larger than that just a couple of days ago. And practically on the beach. Near the south end of Bay Point. In fact, we caught one just yesterday over twelve feet long in the same area." Thinking Mr. Paul didn't believe him, Mikey added, "We sold him to Mr. Fischer for twenty-five dollars."

"That's unusual, a shark that size so near the beach. Usually the big boys stay out. How big you think he was? Maybe you caught him yesterday."

Russ spoke up, "No, sir, he was much, much bigger, maybe twenty feet! Biggest fish I ever saw."

"That's a world-class fish, something like you read about the fellows catching in Queensland. What brand was he, could you tell?"

Mikey answered, "The only shark Russ and I know is a hammerhead. If it's not a hammerhead, we just call it a sand shark. This one wasn't a hammerhead."

"Well, how can I help?"

Mikey then explained the transportation problem they anticipated and the rig they had to address it. "But we just found that a small CO_2 extinguisher costs over thirteen dollars, so we might need to think of something else, especially if we need two. And how can we test fire this setup if it costs thirteen dollars a shot?"

Mr. Paul thought a second, "Well, the thirteen dollars is for the extinguisher with charge. A recharge probably won't cost more than four or five dollars or so. Maybe less. Still, that's a lot of money. You boys are planning to become engineers, are you? That rig you've thought up seems way, way more complicated than you need."

Mikey's shoulders slumped, "You think we wasted our time?"

"Oh, no," Mr. Paul said, "anything you do while paying attention is learning. That's never a waste of time. But let's take a look at the machine. You got it with you?"

Russ spoke up. "It's in the back seat. You want me to bring it in?"

"No, let's go out and take a look." Mr. Paul moved toward the door and the boys followed. Once outside, Russ opened the car door and pushed the front seat forward to reach the tube rigs. The hook and chain were on the floor, and he pulled that out too. He offered them both to Mr. Paul.

Mr. Paul carried the things to a small worktable that was set very near the house. "I've got a hook and chain rig that I think is exactly like this one. It's in the garage there. Think you two could make use of it? You can have it if you want it. I planned to go after shark with it, but I never used it."

Russ answered, "Yes, sir. We just ordered a second rig today down at Fordham's, but we can run by when we leave here and cancel that order. Mr. Fordham might not even have placed it yet. But then we should pay you instead."

Mr. Paul looked directly and seriously into Russ's eyes. "Your money's no good here."

Russ didn't know what he'd said wrong, or what to say now. He didn't know what Mr. Paul meant. Then Mr. Paul's face broke into a broad smile. "I heard that line in a movie once and always wanted to use it. Humphrey Bogart, I think it was. But I mean I won't accept a penny for the hook. It'll be one of my contributions to the adventure. Only I want to be kept posted on the expeditions' successes and failures."

Russ was relieved. "Oh, yes, sir. We will."

With that, Mr. Paul walked to the garage and motioned for the boys to follow. There was no door, just an opening big enough to drive a car in. The floor was dirt. The interior walls were bare pine studs, honeyed from age, sheathed diagonally with 1x pine boards. The place was fairly filled with interesting things. There was a very small skiff on a trailer with a three horsepower Johnson on the transom, the kind with the gas tank as part of the engine cover, without need of a separate tank and hose. The boat contained probably a dozen old duck decoys, each with a length of cotton twine wrapped around a lead sinker. The twine was faded green from immersion, long ago, in copper naphthenate. The decoys and sinkers were hand made. Hanging on the wall there were two cast nets -- both also faded green -- one a small mesh for shrimp and a large net with large mesh for catching mullet and other smallish fish, probably a dozen fishing rods, from light weight rigs with little spincasting Zebcos to long surf rods with medium Penn reels to a pair of heavy boat rods rigged with huge Penn Senators that looked to be nine or ten inches in diameter and fitted with harness eyes. Both boys recognized the big Penns from fishing magazines. They'd never really seen one though until now. There were three bamboo-handled gigs. Stowed neatly in wooden boxes, there were several nets of different types, a seine, a gill net and a small trawl net, the size that can be pulled using just a large outboard. And there, as promised, was the shark rig, looking like new.

Mr. Paul took the hook and chain off the wall and handed it to Mikey. Russ asked, "What sort of rig did you catch the big hammerhead on. Seems like this would have been ideal."

9. THE STORY OF SOLO

Mr. Paul's expression became distant. In a moment he spoke, "I said that hammerhead was off Miami, but I remember now it was Panama, on the Pacific side. I fished there a lot just before the War, with a friend from right here in Beaufort. Gene Davis. He's dead now. When I hooked that hammerhead we were looking for the world's largest sailfish. For nearly a month we fished, every time his boat wasn't chartered. Back then Gene was running a custom sportfisher named *Mary, Mary.* Owned by some rich Yankee, like most of those boats seem to be, or did back then anyway. A beautiful thing. No corners cut. Fifty feet of perfection.

Gene claimed he'd seen -- several times -- the world's largest sailfish. He swore it was twice the size of any sail ever caught. Huge. Now, you don't just see sailfish every day, like you might a mud minnow or a mullet. To have seen this fish at all was odd; to have seen it several times was more odd yet. And recently. When we started our quest, he'd seen it only days before. That was maybe the fourth or fifth time he'd seen it. Or so he claimed. Well, he talked me into pretty nearly believing in this creature; I had my doubts it was real, but Gene didn't have a puff of hot air in him, so I figured the fish might really be out there. Life on the *Mary, Mary* was not bad, as you can imagine. He didn't have to twist my arm. We named the fish Solo, since he was one of a kind and since he likely was a loner."

Russ interrupted. "That's funny, we named our shark."

"You did, huh; what's his name?"

"Hugo. We thought it was kinda scary." Russ thought a second, then added, "For some reason."

Mr. Paul agreed, "Hugo. That strikes me as sort of scary, too. For some reason."

That brought a smile to Russ's face. He was still a little uneasy from "your money's no good."

Mikey asked, "But what happened to Solo? Did you ever catch him?"

"Well, after we'd been fishing for him maybe a month, I got a chance to fish with a well-to-do friend off the coast of Venezuela, keeping the boat -- another high-dollar custom sportfish, but not as nice to my eye as *Mary, Mary* -- in Port-of-Spain, Trinidad. Well, not to say anything against Panama, but Trinidad for a young man is heaven on earth. The ladies... Well, you fellas likely have no interest in girls. Anyway, I left without ever seeing this Solo myself, and away from my friend and his belief in the fish I began to doubt it even existed. It was probably a year before I saw Gene again. We were here in Beaufort. He said he had indeed hooked Solo. He and a Panamanian friend, also a charter boat skipper, had continued to hunt the fish after I left. And they'd found him, and hooked him. He'd seen the fish when he leapt clear of the water, so there was no doubt it was him. Gene said he'd fought the fish for not much more than an hour when something -- it had to have been a large shark -- hit the fish. It was swimming deep at the time, and there was a single violent strike and then nothing. When Gene reeled in there was nothing but braid. The rig was gone."

"Man," Russ said, "too bad. You think your friend was right, though, that it was Solo?"

"Absolutely. Gene was a fisherman since he was a boy younger than you two. And like I said, never prone to exaggeration. If he told you something, you could count it true. He was more upset at losing Solo than I would have thought he might be. Sure, it would have been a feather in his cap to reel in a record, but it seemed like more than that to him. He'd been close to record catches a number of times, but never number one. I'm sure it would have meant a good deal to him. But it was more than that somehow. I never thought of it until today, but now I do, I don't think he ever really cared for fishing again, not like he had before. He needed to make a living, of course, and his reputation kept him employed, but I think much of the thrill was gone after that."

Russ seemed lost in thought. "So you finally believed Solo was real? That he'd just gotten eaten by a shark?"

Mr. Paul thought a few seconds before answering. "Yep, Solo was real, I'm sure."

Mikey spoke up now, "So, Mr. Paul, you think our shark might be real too, despite the crazy size."

10. THE COELACANTH

M r. Paul didn't hesitate. "I do. Don't expect that opinion to be seconded by any ichthyologist. An ichthyologist is a fish scientist. The fish is too big to fit their ideas. They've got plenty of records that say it can't be that big. But have either of you boys ever heard of the coelacanth?"

Both boys just looked puzzled.

"Well, the coelacanth is a fish, about six feet long that was known only from fossil records. It was thought to have gone extinct fifty to a hundred million years ago. Until recently. About ten years back some fisherman pulls up a living coelacanth off the coast of Africa! Every year dozens of fish species are discovered that no one knew existed. I believe more coelacanths will be discovered. I would not be surprised if one of those is the shark whose black petrified teeth we find occasionally in these parts, sometimes five, even seven inches long. The *Carcharodon megalodon.* Some scientists have put the size of this shark at over seventy feet! One put the size at a hundred feet!"

"Good Lord," Mikey exclaimed. "That's as big as a whale. Surely a shark that size would have been seen if it was still around. You're not saying that you think Hugo is one of those. He was huge, but nowhere close to seventy feet long!"

"He might be a baby megalodon, or an adolescent." Then the old man chuckled, "No, no, I don't mean to say he's a megalodon, only that twenty or even twenty-five feet doesn't strike me as impossible at all. Close to the beach is strange, but I guess when you're that size you can go where you want. The simple truth is, you don't really know what's down there. Nobody does."

"Funny, Captain Charlie -- he runs the *Miss Mary* that buys our crabs for Blue Channel -- said pretty much exactly the same thing," Russ said.

"I know Captain Charlie; known him for years. He's one of my favorite people. But I didn't know you two were commercial fishermen. I'd have been more careful with my exaggerations. But believe Charlie and believe me: it's true. Don't trust anybody tells you different. Now let's take a look at your floatation gear."

They walked back outside and over to the table. Mr. Paul picked up one of the U-shaped tubes and examined the closure brackets with the pair of shackles centered on each. "I believe I see the influence of a German machinist in this piece of work. Look how evenly spaced the bolts are, and how the shackles align perfectly with the wood frames. Nothing catywampus about this rig. Mr. Zoo give you boys some help, did he?"

Mikey answered. "He always does. When I was little I was always getting the cuff of my dungarees hung up on my bike's chain guard and bend it all up. I'd walk it over to Mr. Zoo's shop and he'd fix it. And I almost never had to wait. If he was working on something else, he'd usually just stop and fix my bike. Zoo and his good friend Buddy Lubkin have a camp down on Pritchard's Island, and they spend every weekend there. Daddy and I used to go all the time."

"I know the camp well. Spent many days and nights there myself. Yes, old Zoo's a sweet soul. But now this rig you've got here is something else. It's too nice not to use it, but you won't need a fire extinguisher to blow it up. They make a fitting for inflatable life rafts and such. It's mostly used to deflate the rafts, I think. It's got a screw-off cap about an inch to inch-and-a-half in diameter that sits on a threaded boss. I'm sure they don't sell those things as parts, but we can use the idea and make it work using just plumbing fittings."

Russ interrupted, "But Mr. Paul, we don't need to let the air OUT; we need a way to get it in."

"Boys, I know of two easy, cheap ways to get these things blown up. One, you can use my seltzer bottle and fill it with the valve stem already in place. It uses CO_2 cartridges, the same ones used in air guns. They're cost about six cents each if you buy them by the dozen. You'd probably need two dozen to fill these things enough for what you want to do. It would be a little slow, probably take ten or fifteen minutes, but that's a lot better than the hours it would take blowing them up by mouth, plus you two won't pass out in the process. The only problem is I use my seltzer bottle every night and hope to keep using it until I die. I'm afraid to buy one might not be much cheaper than the fire extinguisher."

Russ asked, "What's a seltzer bottle for?

"Making soda water to mix with whiskey."

Russ didn't ask the particulars, but went on to the alternative, "Well, what about the second way? How would having the big opening help?"

"That way will be more fun," Mr. Paul said with a smile of delight. "You boys are familiar with the reaction of vinegar and baking soda, right?"

Both boys answered, "Sure." Mikey continued, "You think we can inflate these things with vinegar and baking soda?"

Mr. Paul smiled. "I know you can, once we get a bigger hole patched in. Look, boys, one-third of a cup of baking soda combines with one cup of vinegar to produce a little more than a gallon of gas. I think you need about ten gallons of gas to get your shark home, so it's simple. We put about two cups of soda into each tube, wait until the flotation is needed, then add five cups of vinegar to each tube, capping off the opening right away. The cost will probably be less than a dollar, all told."

Mikey seemed doubtful, "Really?"

Mr. Paul rubbed his hands together like he was trying to warm them on a cold early morning. "You boys don't believe me? Let me keep the tubes tonight and I'll make the modifications. Tomorrow we can test them. How about it?"

Both boys agreed, but Russ protested it was asking a lot of Mr. Paul to do all that. Mr. Paul assured them it would be an entertainment for him, plus he had to earn his keep if he was expecting the boys to keep him posted. "But now," he added, "I have the unpleasant duty to tell you that all of this preparation is unnecessary. I'm going to do it for the fun, and I think you two will enjoy it too, but in fact you don't need anything in the way of floatation beyond what you've already got, the two five-gallon cans you plan to use on your lines. Just take the floats off the lines once the shark is dead and tie him up to the two, one forward and the other aft."

Russ looked at Mikey. "We're idiots," he said. "All this trouble for nothing."

But Mr. Paul wasn't having any of it. "No, no, not for nothing, boys. You learned some things and you gave Mr. Zoo a chance to help you out, and I'm sure you showed him your appreciation. And the same for me. Plus, now, the next time you see Zoo you can tell him what splendid advice he gave you, sending you to that living encyclopedia of fishing knowledge, yours truly." He smiled while pointing both index fingers to his head. "After all, Mr. Zoo did say I might prove helpful, did he not? And another thing I hope you learned today is that old people usually know more than young people. That's a good thing to keep in mind. So you didn't waste your time. Far from it."

The boys left Mr. Paul and headed for the hardware store to cancel their order. Russ spoke as soon as they were in the car. "That Mr. Paul is cool, isn't he? And he must be ninety years old."

Mikey did some figuring. "Not that old. He said he fished a lot before the war, but the war only ended fifteen years ago. It lasted five years, so that means he was fishing a little over twenty years ago. He said Trinidad was the place for young men, so he was a young man then. My parents call thirty and forty-year-old people young, so maybe he was forty then, twenty years ago. He might not be even sixty now. Maybe he just looks older than he is. He is cool though, isn't he?"

Russ shook his head, "How in the world do you remember things like that, the end of the War?"

"We just studied a lot about the war last year. In Latin class, of all places. We were talking about the Punic wars, where this general, Hannibal, took a bunch of elephants across the mountains and invaded Rome, and Mrs. Crosby spent more time talking about World War II than about Hannibal. Mama says Mrs. Crosby's husband won all sorts of medals fighting in Europe, that's why she's so up on it."

"Mikey, what's the point of studying Latin? Nobody speaks it. Taking elephants across mountains to fight a war sounds pretty interesting though. I never knew about that."

"Yeah, it was really something. Most of the class is boring, though, about like you'd expect. I don't know why I had to take it. Mama insisted. A lot of English comes from Latin; I guess that's the reason she wanted me to take it."

"That shark Mr. Paul said used to live around here, the megalodon, is that a Latin name, megalodon?"

"Maybe, but I never heard of it. If we were in school I could ask Mrs. Crosby. Seventy feet seems impossible, but looking at the teeth in the museum I can believe it. I think I'll look it up in the encyclopedia; maybe it'll have pictures."

"Remember to tell me what you find out."

11. TESTING MR. PAUL'S WORK

The next day the boys went to see Mr. Paul as soon as they finished crabbing. The old man was outside when they arrived, with both tubes on the table beside the house. There was also a gallon of white vinegar and several boxes of baking soda.

"A dollar waiting on a dime here. You boys are holding up science! I thought I was going to have to run the first test without you." He picked up the tubes and handed one to each boy. The ports he'd installed looked factory-made. The boss was a 2" -by-close brass nipple. The flange inside the tube couldn't be seen, but the pipe was big enough and short enough that the boys could feel inside. The rubber was squeezed between that flange and a nut that appeared to have been fashioned from a 2" brass pipe cap. Mr. Paul watched as the boys carefully inspected the modifications. "Well," he said at last, "what do you think?"

Russ smiled, "Did Mr. Zoo help you with these?"

Mr. Paul drew back and looked at Russ, "Mr. Wainwright, a lesser soul might take umbrage at the implications of that question, but I take it as a compliment."

"Just kidding, sir," he said "but they do look every bit as good as anything Mr. Zoo could do. These nuts must have been made by hand, I can see that, but how'd you do it without tools?"

"Oh, I had tools. See that vice welded on the bumper of my truck? That and a hacksaw and a file was all it took. I had the nipples and caps left from a job I did a while back for the town. Fishing wasn't all I ever did. I was a plumber for years. Remember what I told you about old people?"

"I do and now I don't think I'll forget it. So are we going to blow them up?"

"Whenever you two are ready. Let's blow them up more than you'll need to haul a fish, just to test everything for leaks. I've washered the caps, so I'm comfortable they won't leak. I'm less sure about how airtight the base of the pipes will be, where they go through the tubes. Let's try eight gallons of air in the first one and see what that does. I suspect that's a lot less than they can hold, so they won't be much stretched, but it's more than you'll need for your purpose."

So they set about the experiment. Using a funnel, they put two-and-two-thirds cups of baking soda into the first tube, shook it down away from the opening, then funneled two quarts of vinegar in and capped it off. The tube became alive. The growth was dramatic and within a minute the rubber was becoming taut. Mr. Paul put some dishwashing detergent in a bucket, then added about a gallon of water. This he used to wet the entire surface of the inflated tube, paying special attention to the areas of concern. They discovered only a single tiny leak and that around the washered cap that Mr. Paul had said would not be a problem.

Mr. Paul scratched his head, "You two are probably thinking 'the old man got it wrong,' but you would be mistaken. This leak is so minor it wouldn't let an appreciable amount of air out if you had to tote the shark for a week, so it's as tight as it needs to be." He took the cap in hand and retightened it, but the leak continued. He went to his pickup and came back with two pipe wrenches and tightened the cap using them. That stopped the leak. "You could carry a pair of Stillsons with you if you're concerned about the leak, but I wouldn't worry about it."

They inflated the second tube the same amount and tested it for leaks. No leak showed, not even on the washered pipe cap. Mr. Paul suggested they leave them inflated for a few hours, just to further test the seals, so they left them that way while they went to gather the supplies they'd need for their overnight stay at the camp. Tomorrow would be Saturday.

At the Piggly Wiggly they gathered the usual fare: Brunswick Stew, Vienna sausages, corned beef hash, eggs, potato chips, saltines, a loaf of bread and a six-pack of Coke. Plus enough baking soda and vinegar for the inflation task, just in case. Staples like coffee, rice, flour, sugar, salt and cooking oil were on hand at the camp, as were assorted comestibles like soups (cream of mushroom and tomato almost certainly, vegetable and French onion probably), grits, hot sauce, canned tomatoes, canned juices, and pork and beans.

With the provisions in the back seat, they drove down to the Charles Street red dot and hunted up their whiskey buyer, Reb, a young black man with a bad leg who hung out near the store and accommodated underage and Baptist buyers for a small commission. The boys got a pint of vodka and a pint of bourbon. The purchase of two bottles was unusual; ordinarily they made an overnight trip with just a bottle of cheap vodka, plus the Black Label of course, but this trip was special. Then they drove Reb back to the Piggly Wiggly to get the six-pack of Pabst Mikey had lost to Russ. They would get ice enough to fill their cooler tomorrow on the way to the camp. Ice was one of the benefits of working for Blue Channel. They could load their cooler with shaved ice for free anytime they wanted.

They rode out to the fish market to see what might be had for bait. Mr. Fischer had just finished cutting up a grouper and he offered the boys the head, minus the cheeks, for free. He also had a large spot-tail bass, not yet cleaned, that would have a pretty fair-sized head. He agreed to save that, too, in the cooler for the boys to pick up tomorrow when they were ready to go. He would throw in three or four other whole fish that had been on hand a little too long. No charge for those either. The boys thanked him and headed back to Mr. Paul's house.

Both tubes seemed not to have lost the least bit of air, so they deflated them, rinsed them out and stowed them in the trunk. They thanked Mr. Paul and he wished them luck. They were about to drive off when Mr. Paul held up his right index finger. "I'll be right back." He went into the house and came back thirty seconds later with a scrap of paper which he handed to Russ. "My telephone number, just in case you two need me to bring something down to the landing, or whatever. You might be unable to drag Hugo out without the help of an old GMC and a seasoned assistant."

"Well, thank you. 524 1881. I believe I can remember that. But what's this number on the back, 102383?"

"Hmm... I just tore that scrap of paper off a sheet on my bedside table. That's the combination to a safe full of valuables. But don't feel burdened by it. I have complete confidence in you two."

"Well, I appreciate your high opinion," said Russ, "but I would really rather not have the combination to your safe." He offered the paper back to Mr. Paul.

"Just kidding you, Russell. I don't own a safe. I will often scribble a note to myself on waking from a dream if it seems significant. I didn't think anything of this note, just turned it over and wrote my telephone number for you. I can't recall just now what those numbers meant, or anything about the dream that provoked them. Keep the paper and call me if I can help."

12. THE CAMP

The next morning after selling their crabs and collecting the bait and ice they set out in search of the monster shark. It was a calm, clear morning. Even the last couple of miles, nearing the ocean, there were only the gentlest swells. They set their two lines just off the beach. One, as nearly as they could remember, exactly where they'd seen Hugo, the other not a half-mile farther from the beach. Rather than fish with their rods, they went to the camp to settle in, planning to return after they'd had a bite to eat and Mikey had had a short nap. Russ could go without sleep for days, but Mikey had to nap every day, preferably just after lunch. Tide was nearly low, but rising. The small creek leading to the camp had a number of oyster beds that were exposed at low water, some until half tide or better. The oysters from these banks were all clusters and small, good enough eating, but a lot of work. The better, bigger oysters, the singles, were mostly or entirely sub-tidal and you had to know where to look. There were a couple of locations in the camp creek where the boys had discovered some beauties, and come the fall they'd be gathering them for roasts and for stew.

The camp was situated about fifty yards from the creek on the back of a small hummock that had maybe three feet of freeboard at a neap high tide. The building was placed on the highest ground available, but still a spring tide and a northeast breeze would bring water up under the structure. There was no dock; none was needed. Though the extent of the creek through the marsh was nearly all mud from its mouth to its end, the shore of the hummock was a gradual slope of sand running nearly across the creek's full width. Low tide found only a foot-and-a-half-to-two-feet of depth on the sand side of the creek, but this was ideal for landing, no matter the tide.

Mikey nudged the bow of the Halsey against the shore and Russ hopped out with the anchor and set it above high tide in the vegetation of the hummock. Together the boys toted the cooler and provisions to the camp, opened all the doors and windows for ventilation and a couple of Black Labels for a toast, then set about stowing the groceries. It was not yet midday.

Lunch was eaten as the stowing was done: a can of Vienna sausage for each, potato chips and another Black Label. After, Russ broke out the Reserve and they both enjoyed a fresh, unscorched PBR. Then Mikey hit the sack. While he slept, Russ took the camp's sling blade to the nettles and grass from the front door to the landing site, then struck a propane torch and burned off an area where stickers were taking hold. Mikey awoke before the torching was done and opened a couple of Black Labels, and carried one out to his industrious friend. Russ killed the torch and they headed to the boat, taking a small cooler for beer and a bag of snacks. The bait remaining after setting the lines earlier was in the boat in a crocus sack wet with salt water and stowed in the shade of the bow.

13. GALE BREAK

Tide was up a foot or so from where it had been when they came ashore, high enough to make passable the way out the north end of Bay Point, a shallow cut through the front beach that had been created by a storm and was accordingly named Gale Break. It ran dry at low water but with enough tide saved a lot of time and gasoline getting to where the shark lines were set. The boys were checking the first line twenty minutes after leaving the camp. The grouper head was untouched. The line farther from the beach was missing its bait but held no shark. After re-baiting it, they anchored the Halsey several hundred yards away and began fishing with their rods. Aside from two shrimp trawlers in the distance, there was not a boat to be seen.

After ten minutes, Mikey stood and pissed over the transom. "Black Label's running through," he said.

Russ had suppressed some of the stickers' fire earlier, so needed no relief just yet. He asked, "You think the missing bait was Hugo?"

"No. Probably just a passing smallish schnark. I suspect Hugo will take the bait way down before he even knows he's hooked? A fish that size ain't likely to be skittish."

"You know it's funny, but in a way I don't really want to catch him. It seems like as long as he's been around and as big as he is, he ought to be allowed to go on to the end, you know? Like he's paid his dues."

"Yeah, me too. Still, we've got to catch him if we can. We have to."

"Yeah, I know, and it'll be a hell of a thing if we do. People won't believe the size of him."

About four in the afternoon a wind got up. A little unusual for a summer afternoon, it was from the west, but wasn't warning of the squalls so common in the afternoons that time of year, just wind. Tide was by now near full high. Passage through the Break would be clear and easy. The boys decided to call it a day. They checked both the "big lines," found nothing had touched either, and headed for the camp.

Once there, Mikey set out a stern anchor -- a little 2-1/2 pound Danforth -- to keep the Halsey in the water at low tide, and they walked to the camp.

"You did a job on those nettles, Russ. We could be barefoot and not get stuck." The path from the landing area to the camp was fairly clear of any living vegetation. Only black ash and blackened nubs of plants remained in the dry white sand that was the hummock's ground.

Mikey opened a can of Brunswick stew and put it in a pot on the stove, then started a pot of rice. Russ cracked open the vodka and filled two Dixie cups with ice and Coca-Cola, topping them with the vodka. The westerly breeze continued and the camp's interior was comfortable. Russ set the drinks on the only table in the place, and took his usual chair. Mikey added a little butter to his rice, stirred it once and turned the heat down. He covered the pot and joined Russ at the table, sitting on the south side where he always did. The table sat directly beneath two screened windows with a westerly view. At the hummock's edge stood a lone pine, twisted and dwarfed, among several small cedars, all permanently listing away from the prevailing wind that came from the east off the Atlantic. Beyond the trees stretched miles of marshgrass stirring hardly at all in the constant breeze. Three loud caws announced the arrival of a large crow, which settled in the pine.

Russ asked, "Did I ever tell you the story my father told me about catfishing on the Combahee and the crow stealing his bait?"

"No, did he leave the bait out, or what?"

"No, no, the crow stole the bait off the hook."

"C'mon."

"No, seriously. The old man was using clams for bait -- he says catfish are crazy for clams -- and he was fishing some drop lines. You know, tie a line to a tree limb hanging over the water and let the limb do the work. Only when he checked his lines after being gone a little while some were missing their baits, but not a single catfish. The old man was pissed. He was sure somebody had robbed his lines. So he re-baited and left, but went to the backside of the island where his lines were set and walked across to catch the thief. I don't know if he planned to leap from the low bluff into the thief's boat or what, but anyway when he got in sight of his lines he saw a crow sitting on one of the limbs where a line was set. The old man swears this is true. That scoundrel would reach down with his beak, grab ahold of the line, pull it up as far as he could, then stand on it and do it again, until he had the baited hook. Then he'd gobble the clam and move on to the next line. Apparently, he'd seen the old man setting the lines, then waited until he left and gone to work. Crows are crazy for clams too, I guess."

"I've always heard crows were smart, but that's amazing. Good thing they don't have thumbs, they'd rule the world."

"Thumbs?"

"Yeah, Mama told me that scientists believe one of the main things that caused man to come to rule the world was that we have thumbs, so we can handle things better; make weapons and stuff."

"Okay," said Russ as he worked the thumbs of both his hands.

When the rice was ready, Mikey served up two plates of it covered with Brunswick stew. Russ opened a couple of the Pabsts and they ate until all the stew was gone. The camp had a gutter system that filled an elevated tank so there was usually water for cleaning or, after boiling, for drinking in a pinch. Russ washed the dishes and put them away. It was still early, the tide was yet fairly high, though going out, so they decided to check the big lines again before getting very far into the whiskey.

They made the trip out through Gale Break and had checked both lines within a half-hour of leaving the camp. Neither showed any sign of shark and the trip had taken so little time they were able to make it through Gale Break on their return trip. They set the little Danforth as a stern anchor and set the main anchor in the sand and grass above high water.

14. FLORIDA SHARK ATTACK

Back at the camp, Russ got out his Silvertone transistor radio, always tuned to WAPE, Jacksonville, 690 on the AM dial, and they listened to rock 'n' roll while they drank. The news that afternoon included an item that caught their attention. A tourist swimming at St. Augustine Beach had been attacked and killed by what witnesses said was an extremely large shark. Its size was variously estimated at upwards of fifteen feet in length. As yet, no remains had been found. It was the first shark attack in the area in over twenty years. One witness was a specialist in underwater photography working for the Navy. He was in the water very near the victim when the attack occurred. He said that without doubt the shark was a great white. If so, this would be the first reported sighting ever of that top predator near the beaches along Florida's coasts, Atlantic or Gulf. Dr. Oliver Price, a marine biologist specializing in shark behavior at the University of South Florida's marine studies department, warned that nearby beaches should be closed to swimming for a week. He recommended closing beaches from Jacksonville to Flagler Beach. "The great white is widely distributed throughout the oceans of the world," he said, "but it does tend to favor cooler waters. Very likely the fish will be well north of Jacksonville within a week's time."

As the news moved on to other topics, Russ turned the volume down. "This must be some sort of special year for sharks. We see Hugo, then catch the largest shark we've ever caught, and now this."

"Well, if the scientist is right, we might get to see this very shark."

"Or maybe see him again."

"What, you're thinking this white shark might be Hugo? It's possible, I guess, but that would mean he travelled in the wrong direction. When we get home, we need to go to the library and see if we can find some pictures of a great white. Maybe they have something weird about their looks, and maybe we will remember the same look on Hugo. I doubt it, though; he looked like a regular shark to me. Plus, he's way over fifteen feet long."

"But watching someone getting eaten would probably mess up your measurement."

"Yeah, that's true."

Russ poured two vodkas with coke and both boys sat at the table, WAPE still playing on the Silvertone. Russ said, "Hey, when Old Man Paul said we probably didn't care about girls, I expected you to mention Nancy Nicholson. Or have you given up on her?"

"No, but I might as well. She barely knows I exist. If it weren't for hanging out with Tom from time to time, I'd never see her except in the halls during the school year."

"Well, ask her to the YMCA dance next week."

"Please. First, I can't dance; second, I don't like YMCA dances; third, and most important, I don't have the nerve to ask her on a real date."

"Faint heart never kissed the cook."

"What?"

"It's what my old man always told my brother Bobby whenever he couldn't get up the nerve to ask a girl out. Besides, you don't know, she might like clumsy anti-YMCA types."

"Not likely."

"Ask her somewhere else then. To the drive-in. Take my car. It's no Corvette, but it's reliable."

"Russ, this liquor's gettin' to you, man: there is no way that her parents are going to let her go out alone with me after dark. Especially to the drive-in. Besides, Nancy has her license so her old man must know I can't legally drive after dark."

"C'mon, Mikey, you just have to convince them you have high motives. You're attracted to her angelic face and the purity of her soul. That you've never even noticed her butt..."

"Hey, don't talk about Nancy that way. I AM taken with her beautiful face."

"Of course, all I'm saying is that you've got to put Mr. Nick's mind at ease about your intentions. You've got to play down the physical. Or don't play it down, really, ignore it; play up the spiritual. Maybe you could take her to Church one Sunday."

"Man, what kind of turkey do you take me for?"

"But the Church invite would reassure them you can be trusted. Then just take her to the beach instead."

"Hey, that could work. I guess we could just walk along the beach in our Sunday clothes. I could never get her to take her bathing suit in her purse; that would require her agreeing to lie to her parents and she would never do that. I'd have to talk her into the beach as we're heading to church. Or even after! That would seem natural."

"Too bad you couldn't get her to take her bathing suit, though. She really does have a beautiful behind."

"Boy, she does, doesn't she?"

15. TERRESTRIAL MATTERS

From there, the conversation moved on from plotting to use churchgoing as a ruse to less spiritual matters, each vodka refill seeming to take things a notch lower. By the time the Bourbon was opened, things had gotten downright terrestrial.

There was talk of building a barge, rigging it with a winch and recovering the sunken cypress logs littering the bottom of the Savannah River. They would live aboard between trips to shore to market their finds, killing or catching most of their food, laying in a supply of flour, salt and whiskey when they went to the hill.

Russ liked the idea. "But why not go a step further. We can make our own whiskey. Set up a still in the cypress, not far from the river shore. Any high place. We could get a couple of hundred-pound propane bottles for fire. Take one to refill while the other did the cooking."

Mikey chimed in, "We could get Reb to sell our stuff -- whatever we didn't drink. Easy money."

"We'd need handguns. Poachers might be a problem, and boars definitely would be. They're bad all up and down the river. And it takes a lot to kill them. We could get .44 magnums; that would do it."

"Yeah," Mikey said, "and no women would be allowed on the rig. Not even Nancy. They all talk too much. No surer way to get yourself caught by the law than to let a woman know what you're up to." Mikey said he would visit Nancy from time to time, always on no notice, showing up tanned and disheveled, take her out to a fancy restaurant, money no object, then vanish as mysteriously as he'd appeared, leaving her with fond memories and a fluttering pulse. Ah, for the boys danger would abound, but life would be good.

The next morning the boys felt a little fuzzy, but not too bad. Mikey scrambled some eggs and fried up a can of corned beef hash, keeping it cooking until it developed a crisp brown crust on the underside. Russ made the coffee. They both drank lots of ice water.

In the night the wind had died and the camp was beginning to heat up by the time breakfast was eaten. It was maybe eight o'clock when the boys cast off. Tide was ebbing, but was still half high; there was time to make it through Gale Break. Neither of the lines held a shark, but one was missing its bait. The boys re-baited the line using one of the whole fish Mr. Fischer had given them. The other line was untouched, but they re-baited it too.

"Could be these hooks are too big for what's taking the bait," Russ said. "It would take a fairly large shark to swallow the hook, don't you think?"

"Yeah, probably seven or eight feet at least."

They anchored about midway between the two big lines, baited up, opened two Black Labels, and prepared for a day's fishing. The ocean was calm, without a breath of air stirring. It was going to be a hot one. Two trawlers were dragging perhaps a half-mile out beyond the deepest big line. One put out a light black smoke from its stack, probably a fouled injector or two. The other showed no sign her engine was even running, other than the oddly slow motion all trawlers make when they're burdened with their rigs spread open behind. Most trawlers were shrimping the sounds that had opened a week earlier, the earliest opening anyone could remember. That accounted for there being only the two within sight here on the ocean.

Few seagulls were flying, most just resting on the water's placid surface. They would rise in unison when the power take-off of either trawler sounded reveille, and they would circle the boat hauling back, waiting for the occasional small fish that slipped through the net's mesh under the pressure of the catch. The real feast, though, would begin as the crew culled through the catch on deck and swept all the "trash" through the scuppers and overboard. Most of this refuse was unmarketable small fish, what the birds most liked to eat.

Four hours went by without a strike on either of the lines. Tide passed dead low and began to flood. Within an hour of first flood, each boy hooked and landed a shark, not a big one, but both over four feet. Russ commented, "I guess it doesn't take too big a fish to swallow these hooks."

It was nearly noon now and Mikey was constantly wiping his forehead with his index finger and flinging the captured droplets onto the Halsey's plywood. There were two saleable fish in the boat. It was time to call it a day. They checked and retrieved the big rigs, then returned to the camp to do some housekeeping. As it was not possible to return by way of Gale Break with the tide nearly low, they took an extra while getting there. They cleaned up the place, gathering their garbage in paper bags, and headed home. They stopped at Blue Channel on the way in and took enough ice from the cooler to cover their catch. Nobody was there, but the freezer was left unlocked in case any crabbers needed to ice up for the next day. The boys would call Mr. Fischer in the morning.

Back fairly early, they went to report to Mr. Paul. The GMC was there, so Mikey rapped on the door. There was no answer, but as the boys turned away and were headed for the car, Mr. Paul appeared at the screen door. "Partners, what have you got to report? I was dozing, I'm afraid. A habit of old age. You'll see."

Russ beamed greetings. "Very little to report, sir. Caught a couple of small sharks, but no sign of Hugo."

16. A LOCAL SHARK ATTACK

Mr. Paul rubbed his jaw. "Well, remember how long it took to relocate Solo. Fish can be the damndest adversaries. But did you hear about the Paulsen boy?"

Russ looked at Mikey in puzzlement. "Paulsen boy, no. Jimmy Paulsen? What about him?"

"Attacked by a shark yesterday, practically under the bridge, for God's sake. Sailfish capsized. He was righting the boat when he was attacked. Bill Dowling was on the shore watching. Just happened to be there. He said he'd never seen a shark so big. So far they haven't found the body."

Mikey spoke. "Jimmy. I didn't really know him; just to say hello. Good Lord. What's with all these big sharks all of a sudden? Did you hear about the thing in Jacksonville?"

"No, a shark attack?"

"A fifteen-footer attacked somebody at the beach. Guy next to him says it was a great white shark. Ever hear of a great white?"

"I have. Supposed to be most dangerous thing in the sea. I've never seen one, though. Mighty strange, all these big fish leaving their usual habitat and visiting the shallows."

"Do you know if the great white has any special marks on him. Russ was thinking maybe Hugo was the Jacksonville shark, even though we're both sure he was more than fifteen feet long."

"Well, I've seen photos, but he looks about like a lot of other sharks, maybe a little heavier and with a nasty-mean-looking mouth, like he's having a bad day. Nothing you'd probably notice seeing him from a boat, though."

17. THE LIBRARY

Next morning after crabbing was done Mikey decided to visit the library and see if he could find a picture of a great white. Russ decided to go too. He normally would not visit the library -- had never checked out a book, in fact -- but the great white was something he wanted to see. Plus the megalodon. The day was clear and hot. Russ parked in the first space on Craven Street west of Carteret. Mikey put a nickel in the parking meter and the boys went up the front steps into the second story library, the adult library. The children's library was on the first floor, partially below ground level and was entered by a back door. Adult reference works were kept upstairs, along with books and magazines unlikely to appeal to children or young teens. Both upstairs and down were deliciously cool from air conditioning, a feature of a growing number of businesses, but still rare in homes.

The place had the pleasant smell of books and pipe smoke. One of the regular librarians was a crippled fellow named Christy who smoked a pipe pretty much constantly. He was at his desk when the boys entered, his pipe in an ashtray beside him. It must have just been set there as blue smoke was rising in gentle ripples through the light and shadow created by the slatted blinds behind him. He raised his right hand hello to the boys, then pushed himself up from his chair, set a crutch under each arm, picked up his pipe while supporting himself thus and approached. He was bald and bespectacled, his skin a tanned yellow and his arms and hands rope-veined. He moved easily on his crutches, having used them all his life.

In a low voice the librarian greeted the newcomers, "Hey, Michael, what are you two after today?" Christy knew both boys; they all shared the same neighborhood.

"We're hoping to find a picture of a particular shark, a great white shark. Have you ever heard of it?"

"I have, I have. Are you thinking that's the kind of shark that attacked poor Jimmy Paulsen? I thought the great white was a denizen of the deep, not a river dweller."

"Apparently one attacked a man at the beach in Jacksonville yesterday. A fellow who was there said he was sure it was a great white. Plus, Russ and I saw a shark off Bay Point that was at least twenty feet long, maybe twenty-five. Huge. We're wondering if maybe it was a great white."

"It might have been, I guess. Not many kinds of sharks get that big, but I think the great white does, if I remember correctly. There was an article on great whites a few months back in National Geographic. Some good pictures, too. I'll get it for you."

The librarian put his pipe in his mouth and moved, a slowed but graceful pendulum, to the magazine section. Mikey went to the reference section and pulled down both the Britannica and World Book volumes containing "shark." He handed the World Book to Russ and took the Britannica to a table. Russ sat across from him.

When the boys left the library they knew some great white facts. These fish were scary creatures. In 1916 a solitary adolescent had killed and maimed a half-dozen bathers in the New Jersey area, even attacking two men far up a small and shallow river. Those attacks had pretty nearly wrecked the summer season for a lot of beach businesses. And that shark had only been ten feet long! Estimates of the shark's maximum size ranged from eighteen to twenty-two feet and its weight up to about three tons. The National Geographic pictures showed the animal to have a ferocious aspect, but only when seen from under water. Other than its scarred-looking conical snout and its fearsome teeth, it looked, to Russ and Mikey, pretty ordinary. The World Book offered artists' renditions of the monstrous megalodon, and some photos of recovered fossilized teeth. The information offered was pretty thin both boys thought, and speculative. How could anyone know how long ago such creatures lived? They had also investigated the whale shark, finding that some specimens approached forty feet in length, but they were vegetarian, so were of no real interest. It seemed there was no telling whether Hugo was a great white or not. Its size argued it likely was, but the boys didn't find in their brief study whether there were sharks other than the whale shark as big or bigger than the great white.

The following week the town was all about Jimmy Paulsen. Game warden boats joined the Marine Corps underwater teams sent out to locate the body. Because the attack on the Jacksonville bather had received such attention, Paulsen's death became much bigger news than it would otherwise have been. Television crews from Savannah and Charleston filmed segments showing the bridge to Lady's Island where Paulsen had been attacked. All the papers in the southeast and all the major newspapers nationwide carried the story. "Great white" was suddenly on the lips of everyone who could read..

Then, on Tuesday, a thirteen-year-old girl participating in the yacht club's sailing class was capsized and attacked by a "very large" shark. This, like the Paulsen attack, was well up the Beaufort River, probably ten miles from the ocean. The searchers for Jimmy Paulsen now had two bodies to find. And the media coverage intensified to a sort of frenzy. More articles appeared in all the nation's big papers, some emphasizing the rarity of shark attacks, others speculating about whether the same shark was responsible for all three deaths, still others offering facts about the great white shark. It soon became widely known that the great white inhabits all the oceans of the world, and that in Australia the beast is commonly known as "white death." That made the creature even more scary.

The deaths were even mentioned on all three television networks' evening news programs. The paucity of facts only seemed to free the reporters' range of observation and speculation. With such an intense focus by so many news organizations, it was inevitable that the politicians would appear on the scene. Beaufort's mayor was the first to show and he declared the county's waterways off limits until the beast had been caught and killed, though his authority for such a pronouncement was something of a puzzle. The district's representatives, both state and federal, made local appearances, offering condolences to the bereaved families. Both the State's US senators gave news briefings to the press and television reporters in Washington emphasizing the support federal entities -- the Marine Corps and the Coast Guard -- were offering and promising such additional assistance as might be requested. Finally, the Governor made an appearance at the small park at the foot of the Lady's Island bridge on the town side, the site of the Paulsen attack. He declared that until further notice swimming would be banned from the South Carolina / Georgia line to the south shore of Murrells Inlet. This would upset many beach-oriented businesses on Hilton Head, but would spare the much more numerous population of such business owners in Myrtle Beach. Closing the State's entire coast would certainly be simpler in concept, and perhaps more sensible where public safety was concerned, but the governor planned on a second term. Such were the difficult choices faced by the career politician. Civilians had no clue.

18. REWARD

On Thursday, the Hilton Head Island Chamber of Commerce offered a $1,000 reward for the shark, provided the stomach contents showed it to be a maneater.

On this news, Mikey became anxious that he and Russ be the ones to catch Hugo, not some carpetbagger from Hilton Head. "Hugo's our shark. We discovered him and if he's going to get caught we need to do the catching."

Russ said, "Well, we could sure use a thousand dollars. We can just check our pots tomorrow, empty the bait boxes, leave them open and move them to shallow water. With luck we won't be more than a week or so."

"No, man, let's go today. Leave the pots where they are and just go. Tide's not springing; we probably won't lose a one."

"Yeah, but the crabs, man. They'll cannibalize one another in just two or three days without bait."

"So we lose one run of crabs, fifteen or twenty dollars. We've got to be the ones who catch Hugo."

"Mikey, we're not even sure Hugo's the shark that killed these people. He probably is, but we don't know. I'll tell you. You go on today. I'll run the pots tomorrow morning, then take the bateau to the camp and join you. Or you can pick me up at Station Creek landing. If you catch him before I get there, you can have the whole thousand dollars."

"You'll be pissed if I catch him."

"No I won't. Really, go ahead."

"No. I'll stay and we'll go tomorrow. It'll give us more time to get what we'll want to take. You're right, what the hell. Let's go tell Mr. Paul our plan. He'll want to know."

The boys went by Mr. Paul's and found him in. "I had coffee this morning with the sheriff and Harold Schein. Sheriff told us about Hilton Head offering the reward. That much money would set you two up in style."

"We want to run our pots tomorrow morning, then leave them open and without bait," Mikey said. "We'll move them to shallow water and plan on staying at the camp, fishing every day much as we can, coming back just for supplies."

"Sounds like a good plan to me. You don't get a chance at a thousand U.S. dollars every day. And I'm glad to see you're going to clear your pots, not leave those crabs to eat one another."

Mikey said, "Oh, no. We couldn't do that."

"I wish I could join you."

"Well come on," said Russ, "we'd love to have you. Plus, you might be able to teach us a trick or two."

"I can't do it. My granddaughter won a writing contest and she'll be disappointed if I'm not at the awards ceremony. It's tomorrow evening. Besides, I think you two have already learned the main trick."

19. HOW TO SUCCEED AT FISHING

Russ said, "We have?"

"You have. Years ago, when I was maybe nineteen, I worked the back deck of a shrimp trawler, fishing out of what is now Bubba Von Harten's dock. There were maybe a dozen boats selling to Bubba's dad back then, but one captain was always the highliner, week after week. That was Charlie Chaplin's old man, Robert. I came to know that Old Man Chaplin was highliner every season, year after year. He made good money, of course, so he had a nice boat, but not as nice nor as big as some, hardly any better than the one I was working on. But he caught way more shrimp than we did.

"One day I was on the dock and Captain Robert was on the back deck of his boat mending nets. I walked over to where I could talk to him and asked if he knew some secret the other captains didn't know that accounted for his always being the dock's top producer. He paused in his work and thought a second. 'Well, Everett," he said, 'I guess I do have a sort of secret.' I could hardly believe he was about to impart this piscatorial wisdom to me, a teenage deck hand, and I remember wishing I had a pencil and paper. It wasn't necessary. He looked up at me on the dock there and said, 'Everett, if you want to catch a lot of shrimp, you've got to drag the nets.' That was it. You see, the other captains, to a man, found excuses not to leave the dock: the weather was uncertain; they didn't feel 100%; they were short a deckhand; others were reporting poor catches. But not Captain Robert. He fished every day, all day. The only reason he was at the dock that day was that he was waiting on a fuel delivery.

"Now you boys are going out to spend all day every day in search of Hugo. You've learned the secret to success in fishing. I can't tell you anything more important than that."

"Hey, but Mr. Paul," said Russ, "we could pick you up Sunday morning at Station Creek landing. If you didn't feel like staying over, we could drop you back off after we're done fishing for the day, or you could stay over as long as you could stand our cooking."

"I'm grateful for the invite, boys, but you two don't need an old man tagging along. Tell me just where the camp is, though, and I might take my little duck boat down for a visit, if the weather's right."

"That would be great. If you're in Morse Island Creek heading towards Trenchards, our camp is on the right, the last little creek before you get to Gale Break. If the tide's high, you can see it across the marsh from probably a half-mile down before you reach our creek. You know you could use our bateau for the trip, in case your duck boat hadn't been run in a while and might not want to start. We're pulling it up in the marsh at Bill Kennedy's landing. It would be a lot longer trip coming down all the way from town, but the motor runs every day; it starts on the second pull every time."

"Well, if you boys don't mind, I just might use your boat in preference to my own. If the weather's good, it'll be a nice trip. And if it's not good I'll not be coming anyway. In any case, though, I'll check your boat every day to make sure its okay. Any peculiarities about the rig I ought to know about?"

Mikey spoke up, "The motor runs great. We've never needed to change one once, but there are shear pins and cotter keys in a drawer under the back seat. And a few tools, not much. One thing: since we keep it on a buoy, there's only one small navy anchor in the boat -- it's in the bow -- so if you've got another one, bring it. It will make anchoring at the camp a lot easier."

20. HUNTING HUGO AGAIN

The boys took their leave then and went shopping for supplies.

The next morning, the pots were run, emptied and set, open and without bait, in shallow water. They met Miss Mary and squared up. They wrote notes to their parents and slipped them under their front doors. Normally this wouldn't be necessary, but with all the shark mayhem the boys knew the parents would balk at the idea of a shark hunting trip, especially one of indeterminate duration. They headed for the camp well before noon.

By lunchtime the two big lines were set and the boys were fishing with their swing-chain-leadered rigs. They fished the afternoon without a strike, then checked the big lines and retired to the camp for dinner and a night's rest.

The next morning was the same: not a strike and no evidence the big lines had been hit either. They decided to take lunch at the camp; Mikey wanted to nap. When they returned to their spot after lunch, tide was nearly full high. Russ had a strike from something fairly large but it spit the hook. "It moved like a shark," observed Mikey. "Maybe a six or seven-footer from the way he was pulling. It would have paid for a trip to town and a few groceries."

The day ended with no more action and Russ expressed his frustration, "I wish Old Man Paul were here. He might have some ideas. Maybe Hugo's up the river; maybe we're in the wrong place entirely."

"Yeah, maybe. Well, we've only got three more large bait fish, why don't we pull one of the big lines and set it in deep water near the channel buoys. Put it out there now and tomorrow we can anchor near it and fish the deep water ourselves. For a while anyway. We're going to have to go to town tomorrow whether we catch something we can sell or not. We'll be out of ice. And bait."

21. MR. PAUL VISITS THE CAMP

So the line was pulled and set with fresh bait a few hundred yards north of the entrance buoys of Port Royal Sound's shipping channel. Tide was nearly low by the time the boys rounded the last bend in the creek leading to the camp. Russ let out a whoop, "It's our bateau! Old Man Paul made it!"

As they neared the beach off of which the bateau was perfectly positioned -- Mr. Paul had remembered to bring a second anchor -- they saw the old man approaching from the camp. He was with a big black fellow. As the two drew near the black man flashed his signature grin and revealed his gold tooth. "Charlie," yelled Russ, "you're the last person I figured to see down here."

"Well, I miss seeing you two. Makes my trip less enjoyment, more a job. Then Everett comes by out of the blue saying he's going to your camp, see if you hadn't caught the killer leviathan. How could I resist? You boys got a nice spot here, real nice."

Mr. Paul took the anchor Russ had thrown ashore and set it above high water. Mikey had set the stern anchor as they approached the shore. With the boat secure, the boys pulled the bow to the sandy shore and got out. Mr. Paul pointed to the bateau. "That twenty-five never missed a lick. We got here hours ago, went to a little spot I know and caught a mess of whiting and three nice-size flounder. We cleaned enough for supper and kept the rest on ice in case you might need them for bait. Got a chest full of ice, too, and some groceries. Figured you'd surely need the ice."

Mikey shook his head, "You read our minds, we thought we'd have to go to town tomorrow for more bait and ice."

Walking to the camp, Russ asked, "Charlie, today's Saturday. How'd you finish up so early?"

"Well, when Everett came by last night with his invite, I called Cap'm Dave and he said he'd fill in for me. He's got a good second man at the plant, can handle the cooking. Cap'm Dave's eager to get you two back to crabbin', especially since this shark of yours seems to eat everybody he runs into. He's no doubt hoping I'll be able to persuade you to give up this mission."

"No sign of him yet?" asked Mr. Paul.

"No sign of anything," replied Russ. "I had a strike this afternoon, seemed like maybe a six-footer, but he spit the hook. Otherwise, not a nibble. We just moved one of our lines out into deep water, near the channel buoys. You think that might help?"

"Well, if you're doing nothing on the beach, it can't hurt."

At the camp, the boys saw that Mr. Paul had brought along his whiskey and his seltzer bottle. Both were on ice, and were taken out at once. The cleaned fish were iced down too and ready to go. Mikey said, "I want to see how this thing works," talking about the seltzer bottle.

"Good, because Charlie and I are both ready for a cocktail. You boys got any cups?"

Russ went to a large sheet metal box under the sink and retrieved some paper Dixie cups. "If we leave them out, the mice will eat them." He took out four. "You mind if I try that Scotch? I never had any."

Captain Charlie said, "Give him mine, Everett, I can't drink Scotch myself. I've got a bottle of gin in my bag."

"This is Johnnie Walker Black, Charlie. You sure?" Mr. Paul poured two drinks and gave one to Russ. When he'd sipped it, he screwed up his face and handed the drink to Mikey. "Whoa, I think I'll stay with our Bourbon."

Mikey took a sip and seconded that opinion.

"Well," said Mr. Paul, "more for me. It's a bit of an acquired taste, I guess."

The sun was low and red over the marsh. It would set in another half-hour. A single Coleman kerosene lantern was lit and two coils of Pic set to smoldering to ward off the mosquitoes. Mr. Paul said he'd like to earn his keep by doing the cooking, though the meal would be simple as could be: fried fish and grits. That suited everyone and so the visiting chef was soon laboring, lightly, over the hot stove. The scent and sizzle of the frying fish filled the room and Captain Charlie and the boys sat several minutes in silence watching Mr. Paul turn the fish. Charlie broke the silence, inhaling dramatically through his nose. "Damn, Everett, those fish smell good. They about done?"

"They going to be good, too. Like the old girl say, 'it ain't long now.' Russ, would you look in the cooler. I brought a couple of lemons."

Russ found the lemons and took them to the table where he quartered one with his pocket knife. Mikey was stirred from his gustatorial reverie and gathered plates and silverware for the meal.

Russ neared the stove to examine the frying whiting. "Hey, Mr. Paul, do you think that seltzer would be good with Bourbon? I'd like to see that thing work again."

"It's the best mixer there is for Bourbon, in my opinion. What do you usually use?"

"Coca-Cola."

"'When I was a child, I spake as a child, I understood as a child, I thought as a child: but when I became a man, I put away childish things.' First Corinthians, chapter 13, verse 11. How old are you, Mr. Wainwright?"

"Fourteen. I'll be fifteen in September."

"Good Lord! I figured you for sixteen or seventeen. I guess if you're only fourteen, drinking your Bourbon with Coca-Cola makes sense, maybe even for a bit longer, but try one with seltzer and see what you think. In time, you'll come to like it. Rinse your cup out."

Russ got a new cup and half-filled it with ice, then added an ounce or so of Bourbon. Mr. Paul took the lid off the cooler and handed over the seltzer bottle. "Just squeeze that lever and fill'er up."

Captain Charlie watched as Russ tried his new drink. "So, what do you think, Mr. Wainwright? Coca-Cola's better, isn't it? But I'll take my gin over that brown liquor anytime."

Russ squenched his lips a bit. "It's not bad, really. I could get used to it."

"Everett, did you know that these two own the largest stock of Black Label beer in the county, not counting Schein Distributors, of course. How many cases, Russ?"

Mikey spoke up, "Maybe sixty cases."

Mr. Paul, whistled. "How in the world..."

So the boys told the story of their working the warehouse fire. Both Mr. Paul and Captain Charlie remembered it well. It had been big news. By the time the story was told, the fish were ready, eight whiting and the three flounder. The grits too. Mr. Paul served one of the flounder and two whiting along with the grits and took the first plate to Captain Charlie. "You boys help yourselves. Take the flounder. I'm going to have another cocktail, then I'll eat light. Got to watch my figure."

The grits were nearly gone before Mr. Paul served himself. "Had I known I was feeding the starving, I'd have cooked a few more whiting."

Captain Charlie was biting down on his last whiting's tail. "Man these fish were right. But Everett, tell me what your grandchild wrote that won her the contest."

"Yeah," seconded Russ, "how did the ceremony go?"

"It went splendidly. The contest was sponsored by the Gazette, and they offered prizes for the winner and runner up in each grade, plus a prize for the best elementary, best junior high and best high school submissions. The assigned subject was the Fourth of July. My granddaughter's paper was entitled 'The Wrongness of War.' She won for the sixth grade and for elementary school."

Mikey asked, "What's the Fourth of July got to do with war being wrong? And was she saying we should have stayed under the English?"

"No, no. I think she just wanted to write on war being wrong, so she pointed out that the Declaration of Independence would have made war inevitable even if we had not already been at war with England. That allowed her to use the topic she wanted. She might have a future in politics or law. It was quite good though, I thought. Apparently the judges did too."

"I thought the Declaration of Independence was what started the Revolution, and I thought the Revolution was a good war," said Russ.

"No, the war had been going on some months, I believe, before the Declaration was written. But, honestly, I was surprised myself that the judges gave her first place for a paper that seemed to question the

Revolution being right, but they did. Elizabeth wouldn't say the end result was bad, only that it could have been accomplished without war. Of course, she's only twelve, and she didn't know King George. It was very well written, though, and after all it was a writing contest, not a history exercise."

Charlie had just finished nibbling off the dorsal fin of his last whiting. "Man, I love a crispy fish tail. Anyway Everett, tell your granddaughter 'congratulations' for me."

"For me, too," said Russ, carrying his plate to the sink.

"And me," said Mikey, rising from the table with his plate and silverware. "Charlie, if you're done, I'll take your plate."

"Wish I wasn't, but I guess I am," Charlie handed his plate to Mikey.

Mr. Paul glanced at Mikey and smiled, widened his eyes and tipped his head back the littlest bit, then resumed work on his whiting.

"What?" asked Mikey.

"Nothing. So what's the plan for tomorrow? What time you two heading out?"

Russ answered from the sink, taking the plates from Mikey, "Probably 7:30 or so. We thought we'd check the lines, then fish the deeper water near the line by the buoys."

"Charlie and I thought we might wet a line ourownselves. See what we can catch off that shell rake at the mouth of Morse Island Creek. We'll practically be able to see you from there. You hook something you can't handle, we'll come to your rescue, show you how it's done."

Charlie said, "I think I'll have a nightcap before I turn in. Helps me sleep. Speaking of sleep, I'm glad to see you've got plenty of bunks. I'm too old to take a top bunk; I'd never get up there. And if I did, I'd never get back down. What's the arrangement?"

Russ answered, "We've got extra sheets." He pulled the metal chest from under the sink and took out four sheets.

The next morning Mr. Paul again took charge of the stove, fixing coffee, bacon, eggs and grits. Mikey came in from relieving himself around the corner of the camp. "Man, if you came down with us all the time we'd be fat as pigs."

Mr. Paul served up a plate of everything and took it to the table. "Charlie, get your lazy self in here, food's getting cold. You boys serve yourselves. I don't eat breakfast. I'm going to take my coffee down to the boats and see how things look."

Charlie came to the place Mr. Paul had set for him and sat. Russ was pouring coffee. "Coffee, Cap'm Charlie?"

"Thank you, Russell."

Before breakfast was eaten, Mr. Paul returned from his reconnaissance. "Everything looks good, and there's still a whisper of breeze. Mighty nice. Last night was perfect for sleeping, once that rising tide moved a little air, but I woke up probably around midnight and had a time getting back to sleep. A dream."

22. FOREBODING

A dream about what?" Russ asked.

"About that giant sailfish I told you boys about. Solo. You were there, too, Russell. You were in the fighting chair. But the same thing happened, a large shark hit the fish as he was running deep. You brought up nothing but braid."

Charlie recalled the story. "That was the fish you hunted so long with your friend from Beaufort, here, wasn't it? Down in South America somewhere."

"That's right. Panama. The dream had such detail. I was on the back deck of *Mary, Mary*. Gene had the helm, and I could hear those twin Caterpillars idling their deep confident growl, muted for a moment now and then when a wave covered one or both exhausts, and I could see the salt spray the exhausts spit when they came clear. But something was wrong. There was something dark freighting our trip. I woke up frightened, but of what I had no idea."

"Damn, Everett. That don't sound so good."

Russ offered, "Maybe Hugo killed Solo. Maybe that's the connection."

"That seems mighty unlikely. I don't know how long sharks live, but Solo was nearly thirty years ago. Plus, it was in the

Pacific. He'd have had to come around the horn and that's some kind of cold water."

"Well," said Russ, "the shark expert we heard on the radio the day the guy was killed in Jacksonville said great white sharks prefer colder water."

"Doesn't seem to me a shark that prefers cold water would be hanging out in Florida. Anyway, I don't know. You boys just be very careful out there."

Breakfast done, Mikey cleared the table and Russ washed the dishes. Then they all set out.

Mr. Paul and Captain Charlie anchored just off the marsh at the south end of Morse Island Creek, close enough that they could cast onto the oyster banks that lined the creekside margin of the grass.

Russ and Mikey went around the front side of the island first to check the big line they'd left just off the beach. Russ pulled the chain and hook over the gunnel. The bait was untouched. Mikey selected a large whiting from among the fresh ones Mr. Paul had caught and handed it up to Russ, who had already thrown the old bait overboard. Mikey asked, "What do you make of the old man serving Captain Charlie his meals? Most people wouldn't even sit and eat with a Negro, let alone wait on one hand and foot."

"I don't know, but Mr. Paul ain't most people, that's for sure. Besides, I noticed you carried Charlie's plate to the sink."

"I did not," Mikey protested, then, half to himself, "so that's what the old man was smiling about."

"Huh?"
"Oh, nothing."

23. TRAGEDY

The deep water line had not been hit either, so the boys re-baited it and then anchored some distance toward the island and far enough inside the sound that they could see their bateau in the distance, the two old fishermen barely visible. The earlier breeze had died before they'd left the camp and now the water's surface was slick, with the faintest swell from the ocean seeming to intensify the stillness. Russ was opening just his second Black Label when his untended rod was shocked to life, its tip pulsing furiously and the reel's clicker a siren warning of too little line. Mikey began reeling in as fast as he could. When his line was secure, he moved forward and around Russ to hoist the anchor. Russ had set the star drag for maximum resistance, but still the clicker screamed. Mikey cranked the engine and began following the fish, finally silencing the clicker when he'd applied half the throttle. The boat was nearly planning, heading into the sound, away from the ocean, a course that brought them closer to Mr. Paul and Captain Charlie. "Damn," said Mikey, "I'd like to fire off a shot to get Mr. Paul's attention." But there was no way. Russ was fully occupied and couldn't turn loose long enough to rummage under the bow for the 12-guage, and the same was so for Mikey.

But as they came abreast of the bateau they could see that their friends had evidently been watching and had already pulled anchor and were coming out to join the hunt. Within a few minutes the bateau had caught up and both Captain Charlie and Mr. Paul were shouting encouragement from the twenty or so yards separating the two boats. Then the line went slack. Russ began reeling in as fast as he could and Mikey idled the eighteen-horse and put it in neutral. Mr. Paul pulled the bateau closer to the boys. "Stand by, Russell, he may be fooling you," the old man shouted.

No sooner had Mr. Paul spoken than the line went taut again, this time heading east toward the shore, and the clicker began again to scream. Mikey threw the motor in forward and followed the fish. This course took the boys on a collision course with the bateau, but Mr. Paul got his boat out of the way and the boys passed within a few feet of the two old men. As the boats passed, Mr. Paul called out, "I think you've hooked Hugo, Russell. Be careful." Then the line went slack again. Mikey and Russ were now only fifty feet inshore of the bateau. Mr. Paul called out again, "Careful, he might be tricking you!" and brought the bateau closer to the Halsey. Russell was reeling as fast as he could, expecting at any second for the fish to take off in a new direction, but when his line cleared the water there was no hook, no chain, nothing but braid.

"Lord," said Captain Charlie, "that was some huge fish. I'm almost glad he got away."

Mr. Paul looked about for any surface disturbance. "I think you fellows need a long wire leader. I mean long, maybe thirty feet. Braided nylon is not going to hold up against the skin of a fish like that." They all sat in silence for a full minute, then Mikey said, "I need a beer," and opened the cooler. Mr. Paul shut down the engine. "A Scotch would be better, but I think I'll take a beer, too." Captain Charlie and Russ allowed as how they each might take one, too.

Captain Charlie took an oar from the floor of the bateau and paddled toward the Halsey, then extended it to Russ, so that the boats could be brought together. Russ took two Black Labels from the cooler and leaned across the water to hand them to Charlie. As he did the shark emerged from some depth and struck the Halsey hard just at the foremost extremity, throwing Russ into the water and pushing the Halsey away from the bateau. The shark was on the surface now and it was even bigger than Mikey remembered; definitely more than twenty feet in length, maybe twenty-five.

Russ was just coming up and getting his bearings when the fish turned to attack. The bateau was closer than the Halsey, but Russ didn't at first realize what had happened or how short time was in his predicament. Though on the surface, the shark was behind the Halsey, not visible to him. Russ turned back to the Halsey, now fifteen feet away, while the bateau was within arm's length. He hadn't taken two strokes when the shark's dorsal fin pushed the Halsey's bow around and came straight at him. He screamed, "Jesus, no!" Time slowed. The shark was so much on the surface that some of its back was exposed. Russ could see the awful head of the creature, the protruding rows of teeth as it rolled on its side to take in his torso, to wolf him down in terror. He could see the swing chain hanging from the gaping jaws, swept back against the side of the beast. Then there was a splash between him and the shark and the water turned red. He was hit hard. Next, he was being painfully pulled out of the water, literally by the hair of his head. Charlie dropped him on the bateau floor like a wet doll and leaned over the crimson water calling "Everett, Everett." There was no answer. Laying on the floor, Russ was bleeding from a bad scrape along his right side, where apparently the fish had brushed against him with its sandpaper skin and the file-like leading edge of its right pectoral fin.

When Russ realized Mr. Paul was gone, had sacrificed himself to save his new friend, he pushed himself up to a sitting position, his back against the starboard side of the bateau, his left arm laid limp along the front seat. Charlie looked at him, then at Mikey who had brought the Halsey alongside. "Okay, Russell, look sharp now. Everett Paul is a tough old dog. He might break the surface any moment. You okay?" Russ just sat there, vacant-eyed, his face without affect.

Charlie didn't want to leave Russ, but directed Mikey to take the Halsey in widening circles to reconnoiter the area just in case, but they knew it was pointless. There was no sign of Mr. Paul. Finally, Charlie recalled Mikey with a comeback motion of his arm and the shocked party retired to the camp to gather their things for the trip back to town.

Charlie insisted that Russ lie down while he and Mikey got a few things together. In five quiet minutes they were ready for the desolate return trip, but Charlie wanted to let Russ rest a little. "I've heard of people going into shock from things less horrible than this. I can't say I remember what should be done, but I'm pretty sure keeping the injured person lying down and covered was part of it." He poured a Bourbon for Mikey and a gin for himself and not much was said. Charlie went to the open door and stared west across the expanse of marsh toward the site of the horror. After a minute he shook his head and turned back to Mikey. "A hell of a thing," was all he said.

The two tidied the kitchen and bagged the little trash left from their meals. They had not finished their first drink when Russ came from his bed looking better but still shaken and haggard. Captain Charlie got a cup from the sheet metal box and poured Russ a Bourbon, straight up. Russ took a swallow, then went to the cooler and retrieved Mr. Paul's seltzer bottle, added a little ice to his cup and filled it with soda. For the better part of an hour then they mostly sat or stood in reverie and drank. Both Russ and Mikey made isolated remarks on Mr. Paul's bravery, his incredible courage, interspersed with questions from the boys directed to no one, "why?" And, "He hardly knew us; we'd just met him a week ago."

Then Captain Charlie rose and poured himself another gin. "Boys," he said, "when I first met Everett Paul he was dead, or so near to it I couldn't see any life in him. I was running the south route then and I had had some problems; I don't even remember now just what sort of problems, mechanical, I'm sure. It was nearly dark when I crossed the Savannah River, still hours from Blue Channel. I had a boy helping me back then we called Ras, short for Rascal, I suppose; I don't think I ever knew really.

Anyway, Ras was good company, and he was a sharp-eyed dog. Had the eyes of a hawk, I swear. Ras says, 'Captain Charlie, there's a man over there in the marsh!' This was in January and it was COLD. Below freezing. Well, I couldn't see anything, but I know from working with him that Ras can see things I can't, so I have him take the wheel and head for whatever he's seeing. A couple of hundred yards and I begin to see a faint orange something at the edge of the marshgrass on the west side of the creek. Another couple of hundred and I can see it is in fact a man, or a body in a life jacket. No waving arms, no movement at all. I take the wheel back from Ras then and ease over alongside this thing and Ras grabs ahold of him. The two of us manage to drag him over the side. It was a corpse, we thought. Not a sign of a pulse or a breath. Still, Ras has the idea we should warm some dry crocus sacks over the engine, then cover the body with them. So we uncovered the engine and warmed a bunch of sacks, then tucked them under the body and covered it with a couple of layers, head and all.

Well, before we'd reached Haig Point we began hearing moans from our dead friend. Ras was naturally excited about having revived a corpse, and went about heating more sacks and changing them out. By the time we reached the plant, Everett was conscious and coherent. We'd dried his clothes on the engine, so he didn't have to go home in crocus sacks. He insisted he didn't need to see a doctor, so we drove him to his house. He got out a bit shaky, but under his own steam.

I paid him a visit the following day after I'd run my route, just to be sure he was still okay. He was, and he told me how he'd come to be in the river. He'd been duck hunting with a friend. On the trip back home, the boat had hit something just under the water and it had torn such a gash in the bottom that it sank right there. The foot of the motor was ruined, so they didn't even have time to make it to the marsh. Everett had managed to grab a life jacket and he and his friend both clung to it for as long as they could, but before they even made it to the marsh his friend had gone unconscious and went under. Everett said he tried to pull him back to the surface, but he was only able to hold him a few minutes before his hands wouldn't work. He managed to put the life jacket on, but still hadn't made it to the marsh. Not that the marsh would have been much help. Apparently the wind and current took him there after he passed out. He had called the sheriff right after he got home and reported the drowning, then gotten his son to take him to his friend's house to give the bad news to the wife in person."

Mikey said, "No wonder he waited on you hand and foot. He owed you his life."

"Actually more to Ras than to me, but I'm sure he'd 'of treated Ras like something special, too, if he'd had occasion. He was a generous spirit, without a mean bone in his body. I'm going to miss him, even though I almost never saw him. Just knowing he was in the world, you know, made me smile."

Russ asked, "Captain Charlie, why do you think he did what he did? He hardly knew me."

"I can't answer that, Russell. He seemed to have taken a special shine to you. Maybe that's all it was. Or maybe he felt swapping a life near its end for one just beginning made good sense. Whyever he did it, he didn't have time to think about it. Except maybe since his dream last night; maybe he'd been thinking since then. He must have been, now I think about it. The whole thing was so sudden, how could he have acted so fast if he hadn't sort of planned it. He jumped right into the mouth of that thing, practically down its throat."

24. REPORTING THE NEWS

They put their things in boats then for the return trip. When they arrived back in town, the boys didn't know what to do. They didn't know Mr. Paul's son's name. Since it was Sunday, Zoo's shop was closed, plus, he'd be down at his camp until near dark. Captain Charlie didn't know the son. They found a pay phone and checked the directory. There were four Pauls. The only "Everett" was Mr. Paul's number. Charlie had several dimes in his pocket, so they called the other listings. They reached two people at home but neither knew Mr. Paul or his son. Finally, they went to the sheriff's office and reported the events. The deputy on duty took the information and then called the sheriff at home. "Sheriff, we've got three fellows here reporting another shark attack, can you come in? I really don't know the procedures yet, the Marine Corps and Coast Guard. Okay, thank you, sir. Sure, they're right here; hold one." He then told the three that the sheriff wanted to ask a couple of questions and handed the receiver to Mikey.

"Michael Mixon here, sir."

"Mr. Mixon, tell me briefly what happened."

"Well, sir, we were out fishing for the maneater, hoping to earn the reward. We hooked him, but he cut the line. We were about halfway between Station Creek and Morse Island on the Port Royal side. Next thing we know he attacked one of the boats and knocked my friend Russel Wainwright overboard."

"Wainwright of Coastal Dry Cleaners?"

"Yes, sir, the Wainwright's youngest son..."

"Lord, how old was he?"

"He's fourteen, sir, but the shark didn't kill him. He was going to, heading right for him when one of our friends in the other boat jumped in the way, practically into the shark's mouth. Russell Wainwright was injured by the skin of the shark brushing against him, but not seriously. We looked for Mr. Paul, that's the fellow who jumped in, but we didn't find him."

"Not Everett Paul?"

"Yes, sir, Everett Paul. Did you know him?"

"Very well. A lot of mornings we'll eat breakfast together at Harry's. I wouldn't have figured Everett to be after a reward..."

"No, sir, he wasn't. He and a friend just came down to see our camp on Bay Point. They were doing some regular fishing."

"Well, tell my deputy I'm on my way in. I'll stop by Everett's son's house on my way and break the news. Better, let me talk back with the deputy."

So Mikey handed the receiver back to the deputy who seemed to be taking some instructions, then hung up.

"Sheriff's going to notify next of kin himself. He wanted you to point out where the attack took place. Hold one, let me get a chart." Then the deputy went into an adjoining room and returned with a 1240 chart of the area and had the three point out as exactly as they could where the attack had taken place. Marine rescue and the Coast Guard would begin the search for the body right away. The sheriff would handle that himself.

The boys left the office and stood around outside with Captain Charlie, nobody knowing what to do and not wanting to leave one another. They'd been there ten minutes when a deputy drove up. "What you want, boy?" the deputy said to Captain Charlie. "You got something to complain about, come back tomorrow. We don't take complaints on the weekend, 'cept from white folks." Mikey and Russ stared at the deputy like he had dogmess on his chin.

"What you little girls got to say? Is there a problem here?"

Before getting into the car to leave, the boys told Captain Charlie they'd keep him posted on the hunt for Hugo. Captain Charlie shook his head. "No, boys, don't go back out there. That fish is too dangerous. I've never seen the like of him. Maybe if you had a large boat and gear to match, but that fish is twice as long as the offshore racer. And he seems to know it. Everett Paul died to save you, Russell. Don't let that death be wasted. Please."

The boys promised to give quitting some thought, then got in their car and followed Charlie out of the sheriff's parking lot. Mikey asked, "What do you think, Russ? Are you afraid to go back?"

"Yeah, I am. When I saw that shark coming at me today, I'm surprised I didn't mess my britches. But it seems to me we've got no choice, kind of for the same reason Captain Charlie says we should quit. Mr. Paul saved my life, that's true, but did he save it for us to quit? I don't think so."

The boys decided to continue, but to make what changes they could. The problem would be the parents. They weren't going to go for it. Especially when they heard of Mr. Paul's death. They decided to say they were both too scared to continue. That would be easily believed; it was nearly true. Of course, when the ruse was revealed, there'd be consequences, but fortunately neither boy's parents believed in the belt. Some of their friends were not so lucky. Russ's car might be taken away for a week or so, and there'd sure be some extra chores.

The next day they got moving early. First, they went to the landing and switched boats, putting the Halsey well up into the marsh to keep it from sinking in their absence. They would use the crab boat to hunt Hugo. It was two feet longer and much more heavily built, inch-thick cypress planks instead of 3/8" plywood. They also doubled the floats on each of the big lines, using two five-gallon jerry jugs on each. Hugo was just too big to be floated by one jug, and Mikey's dad had been given a dozen of them, so they cost the expedition nothing. They had to wait until eight o'clock for Fordham's to open.　　　Following　　Mr.　　Paul's recommendation, they bought enough stainless steel leader to rig both their lines with thirty feet of it. News of yesterday's events had already spread through the town and Mr. Fordham came over to offer his condolences on the loss of their friend.

By ten o'clock they had checked both big lines and were fishing the same spot as yesterday. From where they were they could see the sheriff and Marine Corps boats dragging grappling rigs. "I know I just met him, but I'm going to miss that old man. How many people do you think would have done what he did?"

"Zero," said Mikey.

"Why did he do it you think?"

"We'll never know that, I guess."

25. A BIG LINE GOES MISSING

Around midday the idea of a nap was on Mikey's mind, so they retired to the camp. After each boy had eaten a can of Vienna sausage and some potato chips, Mikey lay down and Russ busied himself brooming out the place and organizing the shelves. He took the sheets off the bunks not in use and washed them in the sink, then wrung them out and hung them to dry on a short clothesline out back. He was sitting in the bateau with a Black Label gazing out over the marsh toward Gale Break when Mikey joined him.

"You okay, partner?"

"Oh yeah, just thinking about yesterday and Mr. Paul is all. You ready to shove off?

Tide was nearly high, so the shortest route to the big line off the beach was through Gale Break. When they pulled the chain and hook over the side they found the bait looked about as good as new; it had only been in the water a few hours. They went to check the deep water line, but it was gone. They motored into the sound a couple of miles, then back and over near the north shore of Hilton Head. Nothing. Finally, they went a couple of miles out the shipping channel into the ocean. Still no sign. Russ said what both were thinking, "Maybe two cans were not enough to float him. He was fairly huge, bigger than I remembered him being."

"Yeah, but I sure hope that's not it."

They made their circuit again, a little farther on each leg this time. Still nothing. Disheartened, they decided not to fish the remaining hours of the day, but to return to the camp and start again tomorrow. They would re-position the remaining big line, setting it in the deep water that had brought all the recent action. They started on their Bourbon as soon as they got to the camp. Mr. Paul's seltzer bottle was there on ice, and both boys decided to use seltzer instead of Coke. Supper was more Vienna sausage and potato chips. By dark they were pretty fairly lit.

Half drunk, Russ confessed, "I couldn't sleep last night. Kept seeing that shark, then imagining Mr. Paul's last seconds in the mouth of that thing. Every time I dozed, I'd come wide awake, shaking. I've never been afraid like that before, but it's not a good feeling."

The next morning the boys were both a bit fuzzy, but they managed to cook breakfast and to get underway before eight. Tide was too low to use Gale Break, but a half-hour after leaving the camp they were pulling the beach line to be re-set in deep water. After setting the big line where the other had gone missing, they reconnoitered the area again. The rescue boats were gone. They'd either found the remains or had given up. Both boys thought they'd given up, having dragged the area probably a full day with no luck. There was still no sign of the missing rig. They fished the morning without catching anything worthwhile. Near midday Mikey hooked a four-footer. It was not enough to justify going to town, but if they caught one or two more it would be. The boys shot him and covered him with a wet crocus sack. If they caught nothing else, they would ice him down for tomorrow, hoping to catch at least another his size or bigger.

Around the middle of the afternoon a line squall appeared in the western sky promising wind and rain. The boys decided to head to the camp. They checked and re-baited the remaining big line; nothing had hit it, but fresher bait seemed called for. Then they headed for the camp.

As they approached the mouth of Morse Island Creek, Russ thought he saw something red in the swell not far off the beach. They went to investigate, hoping it might be the missing line, though this was well over a mile from where it had been set. The pair of jerry jugs the boys had used on each of the big lines were bound tightly together to keep them from making noise and spooking the sharks. They'd been painted red for visibility. As they neared the location where Russ thought he'd seen something, a swell confirmed his sighting, the float was two hundred yards off the beach, but was not floating high in the water. Either both cans had taken on water, not likely, or some weight was dragging them down. It was only visible in the trough of a swell, and only for a second, but that should be enough to allow recovery. Mikey maneuvered the boat so as to approach the cans against the rising breeze. Russ, gaff in hand, leaned against the starboard gunnel, ready to try for the chain leader or the built-in handles when the can next appeared. He looked back at Mikey, "Well, a faint heart never kissed the cook," he said. "Let's do it."

On the first pass, the gaff banged against the cans, but caught hold of nothing. Mikey took the bateau around again, and this time Russ managed to snag the chain. When the next swell sank the buoy, Russ was nearly dragged overboard. "This thing is heavy. Give me a hand." Mikey put the eighteen-horse in neutral and came forward, but there was not enough room for both boys to get both hands on the gaff.

"Let's mark it and come back at dead low," Russ suggested, "the weather's getting nasty," so Mikey took some of the cheap black poly rope they kept on hand to do anything that needed doing and threaded it through one of the crab pot floats they kept for marking pots that had become buried in water too deep to allow the float line to be fastened to a cleat and dragged out by the power of the outboard. The trick now was to attach this float line to the shark buoy. No way either boy was going overboard to do the job. They tied this newly made marker line to the chain leader of their only remaining swing chain rig, removing the hook, so that it wouldn't catch on anything, then dragged the whole rig up-current across the anchor line of the big line they were hoping to recover. Once the line was hung on the big line's anchor line or chain, they went back to the crab float and brought it aboard, then reeled in the chain line until only the marker line was hung on the big line. They then tied a slipknot around the marker line using the same line's bitter end and cinched it tightly around the big rig's anchor line. All of this went smoothly. They threw the crab float overboard and retired to the camp. They made it almost back before a chilling rain and wind caught them. They were drenched by the time they made the shelter of the camp. They had planned to drink nothing until they'd recovered the big line, but here was an excuse. They dried off and poured a Bourbon and soda.

26. HUGO HOOKED

When they returned nearly three hours later the weather had cleared. Both the marker float and the big line jerry jug float were on the surface, tide being several feet lower and the current of the ebb tide having slackened to near stillness. Mikey maneuvered the bateau alongside the jerry cans and Russ pulled them over the side. Taking the chain leader in both hands he began to pull the chain into the boat. Mikey killed the engine and watched. "Jesus!" Russ exclaimed, "we've caught the miserable son of a bitch; we've got Hugo."

Mikey looked forward over the starboard gunnel and he could see the conical snout of the immense fish hanging vertically just below the surface. Russ put all he had into lifting the fish, but it was hopeless. "Lord, even Captain Dave couldn't lift this thing. We'll have to haul him into the beach, then figure out how to rig him up."

Mikey said, "I think we just made a thousand dollars, partner."

Russ grabbed the anchor line that was attached to the jerry can's handles and pulled the anchor aboard. He took the final twenty feet or so and handed it to Mikey, who took a wrap around the starboard stern cleat. He started the engine and began the tow to shore, aiming to pull the load around the south end of the beach toward the mouth of Morse Island Creek, and into the water of the half-moon cut sheltered by the tongue of sand that was the southernmost end of Bay Point Island, the same place they'd used to load their catch a week ago. Even with tide nearly slack and using better than half throttle, it still took about fifteen minutes to cover the two to three hundred yards to the shallows. When the outboard began to hit the sand, Russ jumped out with a line and leaned into the load, trying to take the bateau into shallower water. It wouldn't budge. Mikey killed and raised the engine and got out to help, but still they made no headway. Thirty or so feet behind them, the shark was still entirely under water.

"We'll have to anchor him here and come back at high tide, pull him up far as we can and wait for low tide," said Russ. "Then at least we'll see just what we've got and be able to figure how to rig him up. I think we're going to need our inner tubes and the jerry cans."

Russ tied the bateau's anchor line to the anchor line of the shark rig and walked the bateau's anchor to the beach. The anchor line was not long enough to reach above high water, so Mikey untied the crab pot float-rigged tag line from the big rig and carried it onshore to Russ. Russ tied this to the bateau's anchor. Now, even if they didn't get back before the anchor was under water, they'd be able to locate and retrieve it.

Wading back out to the bateau, Mikey said, "Wait a minute. We can't leave this shark out here, all marked and ready to be picked up. There's a thousand-dollar reward on this fish. With the news of Mr. Paul, there'll be boats out here any time. I'm surprised there's nobody here already. We'd better take him to the camp."

So Russ went back and retrieved the anchor and they pulled the shark into a little deeper water, waiting for the tide to turn to make the trip to the camp possible. It was near dead low, so the flood was not long in coming. Within a half-hour the twenty-five-horse was laboring north up Morse Island Creek, burdened with a load still hidden beneath the surface. The tow went well enough, making pretty good time, until the final half-mile or so, by which time the tide had risen enough to begin flooding through Gale Break. This reversed the current the bateau faced. It was a weak contrary flow at first, as little water crossed the Break for some time on the first of the incoming. The boys were able to make it to the camp creek before the opposing current grew too strong to allow headway. Once in the camp creek they were home, though the going was still slow and their progress was one of fits and starts as the submerged beast hung on this shell rake or that. It was nearly dark when the boys at last set foot on the camp hummock. The tide was not quite half full.

Once in the kitchen, Bourbon was poured with the last of the seltzer and Mikey raised his paper cup in toast: "To the thousand-dollar partners."

Russ raised his cup in agreement, then added his own toast, "To Mr. Paul."

"To Mr. Paul," Mikey repeated.

Russ downed his drink.

Mikey said, "We've got to be sure we stay awake to drag the shark up close to the boat tonight, once tide's high enough. Get him in the shallow sandy area. Then we can rig him on low water tomorrow for the trip back to town. We'll be heroes. Thousand-dollar heroes."

"Boy, I sure wish that old man was here to see this fish. You know, Mikey, some part of Mr. Paul is in Hugo's gut. We need to make sure that his son gets whatever there is so there can be a burial. I doubt the sheriff or the marine rescue guys have found anything. They didn't with the others, or haven't yet anyway."

"Yeah. It looked like they were dragging the right area, but if there was anything left the current's taken it God knows where by now."

Mikey cooked. Supper was Brunswick stew over rice. After the celebratory Bourbon, the only alcohol drunk was Black Label. "I want to be sober to see that bastard face to face," Russ said.

27. REWARD DOUBLED

"We won't likely see him 'til tomorrow morning. Well, maybe a fin."

The afternoon's rain had left the area drenched, but had cooled things down quite a bit. There was no breeze, though, and the mosquitoes were out in force. The screens were in good shape, but a number would come in whenever a door was opened, a fairly frequent necessity when drinking beer. Russ lit two coils of Pic and set one by either door. He turned on the Silvertone and tuned it to the Beaufort station, 1490. "Maybe there'll be news about Mr. Paul." And before long there was a newsbreak, and, sure enough, the lead story was about Mr. Paul. "On hearing of the tragic loss of yet another life to the maneater or maneaters inhabiting the local waters, the Hilton Head Chamber of Commerce held a special meeting today and voted unanimously to double the reward offered the fisherman who catches the murderous beast, provided only that human remains are found inside the creature. Already, numerous anglers are spending their days in search of the shark, thought to be a great white. With the reward increased to $2,000, the Chamber hopes more will be persuaded to join the hunt."

"Two thousand dollars! Russ, we'll quit school and retire down to the Bahamas! Damn, maybe we'd better get the trusty 12-gauge and guard our prize through the night!"

Russ gave a laugh. "It is a bunch of money, alright. I'm thinking I might give most of mine to Mr. Paul's granddaughter, to help pay for her college. Apparently she's plenty smart; I know the old man would want her to go to college."

"Good Lord, Russ, don't you think her parents can pay for her education? And, smart as she is, she'll probably get to go to college for free anyway."

The boys checked the tide's progress several times, and each time they pulled the shark closer to the camp's shallow sandy landing area. It was nearly midnight before the flood stilled. For their last pull, the boys had cut one of the straighter low limbs from the hummock's lone pine tree. They were able to get a four-foot piece from it about three inches in diameter. Russ tied the shark rig's anchor line around the middle of it and they had an effective yoke. With a boy on each side, they were able to move the shark much better than they'd done gripping the rope with bare hands. They pulled him so close to shore that some of his head and much of his right pectoral fin were out of the water. Russ walked down to the water's edge, then waded out to the shark and rubbed the ugly snout. "No wonder this thing cut me. It's like coarse sandpaper."

Mikey stayed out of the water. "I wish we'd brought a come-along; we could probably pull him entirely out of the water."

"Maybe, but what would we have tied it to? Plus, if we'd found something, then we'd never get him back in. That twenty-five ain't up to dragging this thing off dry ground."

28. THE REMAINS

When they returned to the camp, the boys went to sleep. When Mikey awoke Russ was not in his bunk. Mikey thought at once of the two-thousand-dollar shark and jumped out of bed, put on his shoes and hurried to the landing site. Russ was sitting atop the shark's head, staring down the creek. The beast was huge, but it was mostly gone. "What am I looking at?" Mikey said.

Russ turned to face his friend. "Something ate Hugo, man. Something so big it bit through his body in one tear. Look at it."

Mikey moved next to the shark, grabbed the swing-chain leader still hanging from its mouth. Then he put his hand on the side of its head and dragged it along the sandpaper skin, past Russ and to the torn flesh where the head ended. "Jesus! Whatever did this was HUGE, man, huge. All he left was the head; everything else is gone. How can that be?" Mikey squatted at the end of the head and ran his hand over the torn meat. "Jesus, Mary and Joseph!"

"I would say it was a ship's propeller, but a propeller would've have cut much more cleanly I think; and besides a propeller couldn't have done this unless Hugo was chained in place. This was done by a scissor, a set of jaws. You think it could have been a megaladon? Remember Mr. Paul saying he wouldn't be surprised if that monster was still out there, like the coelacanth, remember?"

"Uh-huh. Yeah, this was no propeller. Whatever it was, though, we're out two thousand dollars. There's no stomach left to prove Hugo ate Mr. Paul or anyone else."

"What do you think, Michael? Should we try to carry this thing back to town?"

"I've got a better idea." Mikey pulled the bateau in and got aboard, then motioned to Russ, "Grab the anchor and hop in." With Russ aboard, Mikey started the twenty-five and retrieved the stern anchor. "Russ, how about re-rig your rod with the swing chain and hook."

An hour later the boys were at a pay phone at a shrimp dock on Hilton Head's Skull Creek. A couple of hours more and they were back at the camp with two representatives of the Hilton Head Chamber of Commerce, one carrying a Nikon camera that probably cost as much as Hugo should have been worth. The Chamber members had come in their own boat, a fancy mahogany inboard with what must have been a very large V-8, to judge from the growl. It followed the old bateau impatiently, like a cheetah being led by a tortoise. Tide was coming up, and was about to submerge Hugo's remains, but it was still low enough to display the evidence. The man with the Nikon looked like he'd been surprised by a living dinosaur, his mouth literally hanging open. His associate was at least able to speak, "Sweet Jesus!"

Russ carried the bateau's anchor up and set it, then returned and gestured to Nikon for their anchor. Mikey spoke, "You see what a huge shark we've caught here. It is a great white and we believe it to be or to have been the largest great white ever seen, let alone caught. It can't be proved now, obviously. You see the chain leader hanging from his mouth, the same leader we have on one of our rigs." At this, he held up the boat rod with the porch chain and handed it across to the pilot of the speedboat. "This is the shark we've been hunting for weeks. It is the same shark that two days ago ate our friend and partner Everett Paul. We both witnessed the thing when it happened. Russell Wainwright here was in the water about to be eaten when Mr. Everett Paul jumped between Russell and the shark and sacrificed himself to save his friend. Still, the shark scraped against Mr. Wainwright and tore a good deal of hide from his ribs. Russ, will you show these fellows your side?"

Russ took off his shirt and removed the wrapping he'd made from a piece of clean sheet. The man with the Nikon gestured OK? then took a couple of shots of Russ's oozing but scabbing-over left side.

"There was another witness, too," Mikey continued, "a Captain Charles Singleton who runs a boat for the Blue Channel company. You can meet him if you want. Now it is unfortunate that this fish was apparently run over by a freighter or some other large ship, but we believe this shark -- or what's left of him -- is the maneater that has caused such fear among the tourists, and among the locals, for that matter. We think it would be best all around if everybody agreed this shark was the problem. Since your members will insist on seeing the thing, we should maybe clean up the wound with a machete or a chain saw. Make it look more like a propeller's work."

The photographer was staring at the torn flesh. "It sure doesn't look like a propeller did it, you're right."

Mikey continued, "But with the size of this thing, nothing else makes sense. Try to take pictures that won't show the details of the wound."

The two Chamber men climbed out of their boat and waded alongside the carcass, both running their hands along the abrasive skin. They were fascinated with the beast. The photographer began taking pictures from all angles. The other man took hold of the exposed pectoral fin. Its leading edge was thicker than his arm. "My God, who would believe that such a thing could even be."

Ultimately it was agreed that Mikey's plan should be adopted, but since the stomach contents were missing, the announcement should not be made until some days passed -- maybe a week or so -- with no more attacks. Of course, the members of the reward committee would have to be consulted and would have to agree, but these two fellows thought that would prove a formality. The general membership was desperate to put this shark problem behind them; it was costing a fortune, especially for the businesses most beach-related. The photographer was confident he had pictures that would show the monster to have been a man-eater, while showing no details of the wound. Several more pictures were taken, these showing the two young anglers resting on their enormous catch, the mouth of which had been pried open to display the rows of death-dealing teeth.

The boys were to call the photographer next day to find how the pictures had turned out. If they weren't satisfactory, they would do their best to dress up the wound to look like a clean cut. To that end, they would return to town this afternoon and fetch a bush axe and a machete and a couple of files. Even with sharp tools it was going to be a lot of work.

On the way into town to get the tools they would need Mikey asked, "Do you think we're doing right? I mean, if a megalodon did eat Hugo, then he's still out there and could start attacking people again."

But Russ was unconcerned. "What is the real chance there an extinct whale-size shark swimming around in Port Royal Sound and nobody's seen it? I agree it doesn't look like a propeller did it, but it pretty well had to be that. Besides, we know Hugo's the maneater. He ate Mr. Paul and, remember, Mr. Dowling saw the attack on Jimmy Paulsen. He said it was a very large shark, the largest one he'd ever seen. That's Hugo, man. If he'd seen a 100-foot shark his description would have been frantic."

Russ was persuaded. "Yeah, I guess that's true."

The next day when the photographer was contacted, everything was going well. Several of the photos were entirely convincing; there would be no need for more pictures with the wound cleaned up. They would be expected to attend a ceremony, presenting the reward, but everything seemed on track. Within two weeks, they'd have two thousand dollars. And be heroes into the bargain.

Mikey hung up. "We did it, partner. The money is ours. A little wait is all."

Walking out the dock to the bateau, Russ said, "Michael, I can't get over how you pulled that off, convincing the Chamber guys, I mean. I was ready to give up the idea of a reward. You made them happy to have just a piece of shark. I don't know what to think of that."

"Think of two THOUSAND dollars, and think how lucky you are to have such a partner as *ego*."

"Ego?"

"Latin for "me," or maybe "I," I'm not sure. Anyway, you're lucky to have me."

"Okay, got it. And I believe it, too. So now what?"

PART TWO

29. THEO'S SEASHELL

So the Now What was that Russ and I collected the $2,000 US dollars and became shark-killing heroes into the bargain. And remember, this was back when a dollar was worth thirty-five or forty cents. $2,000 was a lot of money.

Russ gave half his money -- $500 -- to Mr. Paul's son for his daughter's college fund. I had to talk him out of giving it all. He was like that. I gave 500 too, mostly to persuade him to give only half.

Four years later we visited the campsite together for the last time. I had gone off to attend Duke University in Durham, North Carolina, and was home for a weekend. Russ had joined the Army, 101st Airborne (crazy son of a bitch), bound for Vietnam, and we were going down to memorialize our good-byes, just in case. But at the last minute, Alex Paul, Everett's son, came by and asked if we could take his little boy Theo for the day. It was not ideal, but we could never refuse Alex, so we said for sure. In fact, Theo was interesting company, for a five-year-old.

Alex knew we always drank, so that was not a problem. Theo wanted to bring a friend, but we nixed that: we didn't know the friend's parents, and even back then most parents were not tolerant of drinking babysitters.

Anyway, it was October, and the temperature was ideal. Once at the camp, we fed Theo Vienna sausage and potato chips, then left him to his own devices. Russ and I sat outside the camp enjoying the weather and a little Bourbon and seltzer, and waxing more than a little maudlin. Our main topic, as it had been so often over the past four years, was Mr. Paul. Before we'd finished our second drink, Theo came up to us to ask what it was he'd found. He thought it was some sort of shell he'd never seen. He'd held his treasure behind his back, and when he showed it to us, we were both speechless. After several seconds Russ asked, "Theo, where exactly did you find this. Take us there."

Theo seemed pretty pleased to see us so obviously interested in his find. He turned and motioned for us to follow. We both knew where we'd end up. And sure enough, Theo went directly to the sandy landing where the boat was beached. And where Hugo's remains had spent several days those four long years ago. "I saw a crab, and was wading out to see how close I could get to it. I stepped on this shell right here," Theo said, stopping in shin-deep water just behind our boat. "But do you know what it is, Russ?"

"It's a shark tooth, Theo. The biggest one I've ever seen."

"It must be from Hugo!" Theo exclaimed. "He was the biggest shark ever seen, wasn't he?"

"He sure was," I told him. "He nearly ate Russ before your granddad sacrificed himself to save him. Of course, you've heard that story plenty."

"But Theo," Russ said, "you've seen Hugo's teeth. We saved a bunch of them. Your dad has one."

Theo looked at the tooth in his hand. "You must have given Daddy Hugo's baby tooth."

When we returned to town we convinced Theo we needed his tooth for a joke we planned to play on a buddy, but we'd keep it safe and get it back to him. He was okay with handing it over. We didn't even mention the find to Alex, who wasn't home just then, figuring we'd leave that to Theo and let Alex appraise his son's description as seemed reasonable.

We decided I would carry the tooth back to Durham and find an expert either at Duke or at UNC Chapel Hill who could tell us about it. We were sure we knew what it was, but we couldn't believe it.

30. THE FIRST ICHTHYOLOGIST

Monday morning after my first class I carried myself and Theo's tooth to the biology department and eventually managed to track down a young fellow who was described as "our resident ichthyologist." I found him in his office, working on his computer. I'd been told Isaac Kimbrel was doing post-doctoral work on the differences in feeding habits between carcharhiniformes and lamniformes, two branches of the shark family tree. Great whites were members of the lamniformes. His project was nearly concluded, or the field work was anyway. He would likely be several months collating data and developing his conclusions. I stood at the open door waiting to be acknowledged. After a few moments he looked up. "Can I help you?"

"I hope so. I'm Michael Mixon. I'm looking for Dr. Isaac Kimbrel, the shark expert, but you're too young to be him."

Kimbrel smiled at that, then rose to shake my hand. I was impressed: it's not often a person of some accomplishment shows such deference to a youth. "Sometimes I feel that way myself, too young to be a doctor I mean. But life is strange; I am indeed Dr. Kimbrel. You have a question about sharks?"

"Doctor, unless I'm badly mistaken, life is about to get a lot stranger, a whole lot stranger."

"Oh? How so?"

I reached into my knapsack. "I'm hoping you can identify something for me. I'm pretty sure I know what it is, but it's not possible that it is what I think it is."

"Well, you've got my curiosity up. Let's see what you've brought."

I pulled the tooth from my knapsack. It was in a brown paper bag. I handed the bag to Dr. Kimbrel, who was still standing. Looking puzzled, he took the bag and reached inside. When he brought out Theo's tooth, he just stared at it. He sat down, still staring at the tooth. He cocked his head as if to get a different vantage point, to better take in what was in his hand. "Mother of God," he uttered, barely loudly enough for me to hear. "Carcharocles megalodon. This is the largest tooth in existence! The largest yet discovered anyway. By a wide margin. And milk white, as if the creature had just lost it, was still swimming today!" He fumbled in his desk drawer and came out with an engineer's rule, and laid it against the tooth, which he had placed on his desk. "Nearly eight-and-a-half inches! My God! What sediment could have so preserved it? Mr. Mixon, you've got to take me to the site of this find. You know, of course, that this tooth is worth a fortune. Well, perhaps not a fortune, but a lot of money."

"No," I said, "I didn't know that." I reached across the desk and took the tooth.

"I wish you could leave this with me, just for the day, to show my colleagues. But I understand you want to take it with you. Let me get a camera and take some pictures, at least. He got up and left the office, hurrying down the hall. He returned in less than a minute with a camera and asked if I would mind. I handed the tooth to him and he took several shots of it against the engineers' rule, talking the whole time. "When might we visit the site of this find? I can go anytime that suits you."

I explained that I was only a student, and a freshman at that, and that we'd have to go on a weekend.

"This weekend?" he pressed.

"This weekend will work. But in the meantime why don't we get together for a beer and let me fill you in on the strange history of this discovery. Tonight? Tomorrow night?"

"Tonight. Right now, if you want."

"I've got two more classes today. But tonight." I gave him my phone number.

We met that evening at a bar located just off campus, Dr Kimbrel's choice. We both got dark draughts, then settled into a booth. I was only a minute or so into the story of Hugo when Dr. Kimbrel interrupted me. "Of course, the great white that caused such a panic in Beaufort a few years back. Several fatal attacks in a single week, or maybe two. So you're the fellow who caught the shark."

"One of the fellows, yes." I went on to tell him the whole story, the first sighting, Mr. Paul's sacrifice, catching Hugo, then realizing he'd been cut in two by a ship's propeller, then Theo's find and finally realizing that there was no ship's propeller involved, that Hugo had been attacked by a shark long thought to be extinct, C. megalodon. The tooth looked fresh because it was fresh, only four years on the bottom. It had no doubt been lost when the megalodon tore into the thick and tough hide of Hugo. It must have been lodged in Hugo's flesh when we brought him to the camp, and fallen out there, only to be discovered by Theo.

Dr. Kimbrel did not take the story well. He became at first skeptical, then hostile as the tale was told. By the time I told him about Theo's discovery, he was having none of it.

"Mr. Mixon, I don't know what you hope to accomplish by spinning this yarn, but I can tell you that I will not participate in your scheme. I'm sure you enjoyed the fame, such as it was, from catching this 'Hugo,' but to try to enlist science in support of your need for notoriety... It's not going to happen. I would be interested in learning how you bleached the tooth, but not sufficiently interested to promote your lies."

31. LAZARUS TAXON

"Whoa, Doc, what's all this? You think I'm lying to, for what? To get back on the nightly news?"

"That or some other unworthy goal."

"Doc, we can't all be on the government tit, studying why some fish shit where they eat and some don't. Some of us live in the real world, where things happen; sometimes unexpected things. Things like the coelacanth."

"Mr. Mixon, the coelacanth is a six-foot bottom-dwelling night-foraging consumer of small fish. C. megalodon was the apex marine predator of the entire planet, at least 60 feet in length and perhaps much larger than that, to judge from the tooth you have. Such a creature might weigh in excess of 100 tons. That such a monster might be a living Lazarus taxon is beyond ridiculous."

"Lazarus taxon? You got me there, Doc."

"The reappearance of a species thought to have gone extinct. Usually such reappearances are found in the fossil record, separated perhaps by only millennia, but sometimes by ages, even epochs from the specimen previously thought to have been the end of that line, but occasionally -- very,

very, VERY rarely -- by a living specimen, the coelacanth, for example."

"I can see how such a thing seems impossibly remote."

But Doctor Kimbrel waved me off, got up from our table, pulled a five-dollar bill from his wallet and dropped it on the table. Then he turned and left.

I resolved to find an older expert.

32. AN OLDER ICHTHYOLOGIST

The next day I took myself to the museum on Murray Avenue and was lucky enough to meet the curator, a Dr. Boxer. When I told her of my mission, she first suggested Dr. Kimbrel, which was something of a disappointment, but she was not put off by my discounting Kimbrel's fitness for the task I intended to accomplish.

"I might have just the fellow for you, right here at the museum. We think of him as our resident paleontologist, though he's not academically credentialed as such. Actually, he does hold a Ph D, but in physics."

I could not help thinking of yesterday's description of Kimbrel as "our resident ichthyologist," and I began to wonder if this mission was snakebit. As it happened, this fellow, Dr. Everett, was in the museum right then, rearranging a display of pterodactyl fossils. Dr. Boxer led me to the exhibit and introduced me to the man. I felt relief on seeing him. He was an old man, gray and more than a little wrinkled, and he had mischievous eyes, but kind eyes.

"Dr. Everett," said the curator, "I have a young guest who wants to pick your brain." She motioned to me, "This is Michael Mixon; he wants to ask you about sharks. Michael, this is our resident paleontologist, Dr. Everett."

"Please, Beth, dispense with the formal prefixes. Michael, just call me Paul; it will save a lot of breath. But are you by any chance <u>the</u> Michael Mixon?"

"Uhh... I don't think so." I was thinking, this man cannot possibly be named Paul Everett.

"So you're not the fellow who caught the maneater in Beaufort, South Carolina a few years back? You sure look a lot like him, grown older of course. I've got quite a memory for facts and faces, but maybe I'm succumbing to old-timers disease."

"Oh, well, yes, I am that Michael Mixon, but how can you possibly remember that. It was more than four years ago."

"Well, Michael -- it's fine to call you 'Michael,' I hope?"

"Yes, sir, of course."

"Well, that was big news at the time, and especially for me. I'm fascinated with sharks. I always have been. I even called the Hilton Head Chamber of Commerce, hoping I might go down to photograph and measure the beast. I was shocked when they told me they'd disposed of the remains. It should have become a museum exhibit somewhere. People are crazy about sharks; it would have drawn many, many visitors."

Dr. Boxer broke in, "Well, I'll leave you two to your sharks. Work, work, work." She walked away, then turned and came back, "but if you come up with a huge shark -- at a reasonable price and dead, of course -- I want to be the first to know." Then she left again.

Dr. Everett looked after her, "That Dr. Boxer is a wonderful curator. We're lucky to have her. But what's on your mind, Michael."

"Dr. Everett," I began, but he cocked his head and raised both his hands. "Paul, I continued, the reason I've come to you ties in with the quick disposal of the shark we caught. But before I go into that I have to ask you if your name is really Paul Everett."

"It is. Paul Theodorus Everett. Theodorus you may not know was the name of Vincent van Gogh's younger brother. Their father, too, was Theodorus. So I have what many of my colleagues enjoy pointing out, three first names. But why do you ask?"

I told him then about Everett Paul, his dying in the jaws of Hugo while saving Russell Wainwright, and then began again, this time the whole story from our first sighting of the huge shark. When I came to the catching of Hugo and the horribly rent flesh we discovered, I told him we'd put it down to a ship's propeller, but that it didn't look like the work of a propeller, which both Russ and I thought would have been relatively smooth and surgical. "It looked like he'd been cut in half by a shark. It was this concern, I'm sure, that caused the Chamber of Commerce to dispose of the body quickly and without fanfare."

"But it gets a lot stranger, Dr. Everett. Just this past weekend we -- Russell Wainwright and I -- went back to the camp where we'd parked the carcass of Hugo. We took Everett Paul's five-year-old grandson,

Theo -- yes, Theo -- with us, and while he was playing on the sand spit where we pull up and leave our boats, and where we'd secured Hugo for the three days he was with us, before the Chamber people came and hauled him away, he found a strange thing. He thought it was a seashell of some kind." I said that I did not know if Theo was Mr. Paul's middle name, but such an unusual name almost had to have come to the little boy from some family connection. I wondered if a statistician could reckon the probability of such a naming coincidence.

33. C. MEGALODON

The world is full of wonder, Michael," the old man said. "And not a few coincidences. This is a particularly strange one, though, I have to admit. But I'm becoming anxious. I hope you've brought Theo's seashell with you. Let's go to my desk. The museum provides me with a small work space, more a carrel than an office, but entirely adequate." He began walking away from the pterodactyl exhibit, and in a half-minute we were in a room the size of a large closet with a small desk, bare except for a slide rule, a pad of paper and a handsome ink pen, all arranged neatly along the desk's top edge.

"I have brought it," I said, opening my knapsack. "First, though, I'd like to show you one of Hugo's teeth. You can have it; I had a smaller one mounted and wear it as a good luck necklace." I withdrew the one Hugo tooth I'd brought. "This tooth is as big as any were, so maybe it could tell you something of his size. We saw him a couple of times swimming near our boat and guessed he was twenty-feet-plus, but we only landed part of him, so we don't really know how long he was. He was huge, though, to judge from the part of him recovered. We'd caught a twelve-footer maybe a week before Hugo, and the part of Hugo we recovered

weighed WAY more than that whole shark."
I handed the tooth to Dr. Everett.

He took it in his left hand and ran his right across the flat back surface reverently, then along the serrations that adorned both edges. "Beautiful," he said. He reached into his trouser pocket and withdrew a small chrome-cased tape measure about the diameter of a silver dollar and only maybe twice as thick. Laying the tooth on his desk, he measured it from crown to tip along the serrated edge, then the vertical height of the enameled surface and finally the width of the root. He did some mental calculations. "There are several formulae for relating a shark's tooth size to the animal's overall length. Assuming this specimen to be Hugo's largest upper anterior tooth, even the most conservative of these suggests Hugo to have been something over seven meters in length. He was huge, perhaps a record."

"Seven meters is..."

"About twenty-three feet. He probably weighed something over three tons."

"Three TONS? Good lord, the twelve-footer we caught weighed less than five hundred pounds. How could Hugo have weighed more than ten times as much?"

"Well, a shark's weight-to-length ratio increases greatly with the length of the animal. Too, the great white is an especially robust creature, morphologically speaking."

I then pulled the "seashell" from my bag. "Now look at this, Doctor." I set it on his desk. "I showed it to Dr. Kimbrel at Duke yesterday."

The doctor looked at the tooth in silence for fully ten seconds before reaching out and picking it up. "Lord deliver me," he said, mainly to himself, then "C. megalodon. This appears to be the tooth of a living megalodon. You are suggesting that at least one of these creatures is alive today and that it devoured Hugo. It was not a ship's propeller."

"Doctor, I don't know. I do know that both Russell Wainwright and I thought the flesh was too raggedly torn to have been the work of a propeller, but nothing else made sense, and what do we -- or probably anybody -- know about how a large -- a huge -- shark would look after encountering a ship's propeller. It just seemed it should be a whole lot cleaner than what it was. But when I told Dr. Kimbrel my speculation, he suddenly became angry; he even claimed I was trying to whodo him for the publicity it would bring me. He thinks I treated this tooth with some sort of bleaching chemicals and that it was like a refurbished fossil. It was insulting."

"Well," Dr. Everett said, "we can -- and with your permission will -- date this tooth radiometrically. That will show conclusively if it's new, but I believe you."

"If there are ways to prove the tooth is fresh, why didn't Dr. Kimbrel know about them?"

"Oh, Dr. Kimbrel is surely well acquainted with radiometric dating. My guess would be that Dr. Kimbrel, a young man with a bright future, would not want to take a chance associating his name with anything so implausible. It could, of course, make him widely famous overnight, but it could also make him look to be a gullible neophyte, a sucker. He's on course to a very successful career; why take chances."

"But wouldn't this dating technique offer him all the evidence he'd need to protect his reputation?"

"It should, but there's many a slip 'twixt the cup and the lip. You can never be sure how some things will be received. Especially when you're talking about something as outrageously improbable as this. Are you acquainted with the term 'Lazarus taxon'?"

"Dr. Kimbrel explained it to me."

"Well, you can see how it might strike many people more than odd that one of the largest creatures on the planet has managed to avoid detection for the whole of human history."

———————————————

Long story short, Dr. Everett arranged the radiometric dating of the tooth and it was found to be fresh, likely from a living specimen. The publication of this result brought huge exposure to the doctor and to his employer the museum. Arrangements were made for the loan of the tooth to the museum by Theo's father and mother, along with a grant of first refusal right to the museum should the decision be made to sell the tooth. The parents' hopes were, though, that it would remain on loan until Theo reached his majority when he could decide whether or not to sell it. Dr. Everett suggested that it would bring enough to put him through college and then some.

Dr. Boxer pressed the board of governors hard, and succeeded in getting the funds needed to make the megalodon exhibit one of the most impressive in the museum. She commissioned the modeling and construction of a set of megalodon jaws measuring some ten feet in width, claimed to be the actual size indicated by Theo's tooth. A mural depicting megalodon in pursuit of its prey formed the background of the exhibit. The tooth itself was set in a lighted heavy glass case the bottom of which was covered in beach sand representing the bottom of the sea.

Theo and his family were guests of honor at the exhibit's opening. Theo and his sister were especially impressed that the megalodon tooth, or rather the heavy glass cabinet in which it was displayed, carried an engraved description on a large polished brass plate informing the visiting public that the tooth exhibited was from the only known (apparently still) living example of C. megalodon, a creature thought to have gone extinct some one point five million years ago; that the creature which had lost this tooth was calculated to have an open jaw width in excess of three meters ("see the scale model at right") and a weight likely in excess of 125 metric tons. "This tooth is on loan to our museum from its owner, Alexander Michael Theodorus Paul ("Theo Paul")." Theo and his sister both thought this was the best part of the whole exhibit. Theo ran his fingers over the special text dozens of times, often saying aloud, "This tooth is on loan to our museum from its owner, Alexander Michael Theodorus Paul, Theo Paul." Then Theo would giggle or even laugh out loud. His sister Sarah, now sixteen, would smile at her little brother's delight. Overnight C. Megalodon became the museum's most popular exhibit.

PART THREE

34. DEATH OF RUSSELL WAINWRIGHT

Russell and I saw very little of one another after our last trip to the camp. He did two tours in Vietnam, then continued with the Army, planning to make it a career. He never married. Neither did he ever retire. He was killed in the bombing of the Marine Corps barracks in Beirut in 1983, one of only three army men who died there. He was a Sergeant Major.

On his last trip to Beaufort, he and I got together for a few drinks. We talked about Hugo and the megalodon, about Theo and his sister and parents, and of course about Mr. Paul.

Like so many of us who grew up in the lowcountry of South Carolina during halcyon years of the fifties and sixties, I was put off by what the area had become. And this was before the Port of Port Royal was closed because the new residents didn't like the tractor trailers coming through town, or the train whistle disrupting the quiet of the day, though both these offensive happenings were near-daily events long before these folks had taken up residence. In a particularly Disneyworld move, the powers that be would oversee the dismantling of that offensive railway, the area's only working one, to allow for the construction of a bicycle trail, at a cost of over $33 million to U.S. taxpayers. The bumper-to-bumper traffic which was to so degrade the area's quality of life was still twenty years in the future.

But even back then I suspected I knew what he thought of the area's transformation, and asked, "So, Russell, if you had to choose between an all-expenses-paid twelve-month stay on Hilton Head Island or an all-expenses-paid twelve-month regimen of radical chemotherapy and radiation focusing on your privates, which would it be."

He thought a moment. "Man, that's a tough one, Mike."

Word of Russell's death was announced in the paper, and added forcefulness to the sensed futility of our nation's intervening in religion-motivated conflicts. Russell himself had been a particularly non-religious fellow. He left it to others to drink the communion wine or grape juice; he'd take Pabst Blue Ribbon. Still, his brother and mother had decided to have the funeral in the graveyard beside the Baptist Church rather than in the National Cemetery on Boundary Street.

They both attended the church, and Russell's father was buried there.

After the funeral, there was a reception for friends at the church's social center across the street from the graveyard. I had spied a large gold-toothed black man from the pulpit when I'd offered my eulogy, and now I caught up with him leaving the graveyard. He was accompanied by a young man.

"Captain Charlie, it's me, Michael -- Mikey -- it's been years. How are you?"

Charlie offered me the same broad smile he'd had on the deck of the *Miss Mary* all those years ago. He'd aged, but not that much. His hair now was mostly gray, and he'd put on some pounds, but all in all he looked fit and well. "I would be better if we were not here to bury our friend, but otherwise I'm doing about as good as I have any right to hope. Michael, this is my son, Charles, Jr. Charles, this young man is one of those I've told you about so often, Mr. Wainwright's special friend, Michael Mixon."

The young black man put out his hand and looked genuinely happy to make my acquaintance. "Very pleased," he said, "I've heard the story of Hugo more times than I can tell you. As a little boy it was my very favorite. I expect if I have children myself one day, it will be their favorite, too."

Captain Charlie and his son kept walking when they came to the entrance of the social center. "Captain Charlie, you're not coming in for refreshments?"

"Now Michael, you know there's no alcohol in there. I want to go home, sit on my porch and enjoy my gin and memories. Time is short. It was short when Everett Paul was living; it's yet shorter now."

I tried for levity: "Like the old girl say, 'it ain't long now.'"

Captain Charlie didn't say anything.

"But Captain Charlie, I have to talk to you. You know, we never did understand -- at least Russell and I didn't -- why Everett Paul did what he did. And now we hear from the general there that Russell lived out his life apparently without fear himself, even in the most frightful circumstances. What do you make of that? Is there some connection? He was certainly scared to death by Hugo; he told me so."

"Yes, I'd say there's some connection, but what I can't say."

Charles, Jr. broke in, "I think it's clear. Russell Wainwright was an exceptional fellow. You yourself said he was practically fearless even as a boy. Then he's saved by a man who exchanged his own life for Russell's. Most people would just count that a lucky break, and be happy to be still breathing. Mr. Wainwright was better than that. He saw his situation from then on as that of an honest debtor. Of course he would never get the opportunity to repay his debt to Mr. Paul, but he was not going to forget the debt. My mama used to say, 'I'd rather owe you all my life than cheat you out of it,' and I think that was Mr. Wainwright's mission from Hugo on. He owed, and he was going to pay."

EPILOGUE

I made a pilgrimage to the camp the day after Russell's funeral. It had been probably fifteen years since my last visit. The nettles and other weeds had taken over and the path from the landing area to the front door was long gone. The solitary pine and the dwarfed cedars were still there, not much changed in all that time. The scar that was the site of the pine's missing low limb, the one we'd used as a yoke to drag Hugo, was a moldy gray-black now and the resin that had bled from the wound had hardened as a milky translucence years ago. But otherwise the trees were healthy and very little larger than I remembered them to have been.

The camp was another matter. Only remnants of the screens survived. The plywood siding was bleached gray and the south side was covered in mildew. At the seams there were signs of delamination. The front door was still in place, though, securely closed by a 16-penny galvanized common nail bent in a U and hanging in the hasp that had always served as the outside lock when the camp was not in use. Inside, a leak had developed in the roof and rainwater had rotted the floor of the kitchen near the sink. But the propane cookstove was still there, and the table set beneath the two westward-facing windows. The chairs were ready to support diners, and I took my place where I'd always sat those many years ago. In a minute I could see things as they had been on that special night. Mr. Paul was turning fish in the pan and Captain Charlie was watching his progress. Russ was setting the table. There was the sense then, for me at least and I suspect for Russ too, though it was never articulated, that everything was within our reach, that we were at home in the world, and that we pretty much had that world by the tail.

I had brought a flask of Scotch to toast my dead friend, and I removed it now from my jacket pocket. I'd also brought a paper bag containing several items given me just yesterday by Bobby Wainwright, Russell's brother. "There's nothing much here; probably the only thing you'll want is a small framed photo of you two back in your crabbing days. He took it with him all over the world. There are two bullets that I figure must have been removed from his tough hide. He was shot more than a few times, but most times the bullets just passed right through, I'm sure. There are a couple of things from his wallet that might mean something to you. If not, don't hesitate to throw them away. Mama has plenty to remember him by."

I emptied the bag on the table and picked up the photo. There were the two of us in the old bateau. We were shirtless, as we nearly always were when we were crabbing. This was the summer of Hugo, but before we'd seen him. We'd finished running the pots and we'd done well. Baskets of crabs stacked two deep fairly covered the bottom of the boat. We were both standing, Russ near the bow and me at the old green twenty-five-horse. Russ had donned his orange rubber gloves for the shot. My memory created these colors; the photo was black-and-white. I remembered the day the picture had been taken. *Miss Mary* was late and Russ and I had run to the Halsey landing in order to move the boat into deeper water, fearing it might be caught by the outgoing tide and wreck our schedule for going to the camp. There was a fellow on the shore there, a tourist taking pictures of the local color. We talked briefly and he asked if we'd mind getting our pictures taken. Of course we didn't mind, and he took several of us. He asked our names, for his photo album he said. Some weeks later the postman delivered an envelope to Russ's house, addressed to Russell Wainwright, Beaufort, South Carolina. Back then, that's all that was necessary.

The bullets looked like those from military rounds, about 30 caliber and full metal jacket.

There were two things that must have been from his wallet. Both were laminated in protective plastic and so had survived in good shape. The first was a pale blue sheet that was folded to allow nearly its entire front to be read by turning the laminate over. It was Russell's first hunting license, issued on his fourteenth birthday. He'd been five-foot-six then and weighed 115 pounds. No wonder we had such a struggle loading that first big shark.

The second, though, fairly took my breath away. It was a scrap of white paper bearing a telephone number, 524 1818. Mr. Paul's number, written in the old man's hand. I remembered him handing it to Russell as we prepared to leave his yard to hunt for Hugo. Considering how their lives had been joined, it was not surprising that Russ would want to carry this personal artifact. But it was the reverse that kept me staring hard at the laminated scrap. Written also in the old man's hand were the numbers 102383. Mr. Paul had told us it was the combination to a safe full of valuables, then that he was joking, that he didn't own a safe, and that he couldn't recall what the numbers meant. It might, of course, have been pure coincidence, but I was sure it was not. 102383. 10 23 83. October 23rd, 1983. The day of the Marine Corps barracks bombing in Beirut. The day of Russell Wainwright's death.

I wished then my flask of Scotch was bigger. I unscrewed the silver cap and raised it. "To my special friend, Russell Wainwright." I put the flask to my lips and took a big pull. In a moment I raised the flask again. "To Mr. Paul." Another big pull. The weight of the flask suggested there was but one big swallow remaining. I raised the flask. "To better times."

If you enjoyed this book I would be very grateful if you would post a positive review. Your support matters, and I do read all reviews so I can get your feedback.

If you'd like to leave a review all you need to do is go to the review section on the book's Amazon page. You'll see a big button that says "Write a customer review;" click that and you're good to go.

Thanks again for your support.

Michael McEachern

Michael McEachern has lived in the lowcountry of South Carolina all his life. He lived many chapters of the story offered here with Russell P, a boyhood friend and neighbor.